A LENAPE CAPTIVE

AHMEYA

DORIS WILBUR

MILFORD
HOUSE

an imprint of Sunbury Press, Inc.
Mechanicsburg, PA USA

MILFORD HOUSE

an imprint of Sunbury Press, Inc.
Mechanicsburg, PA USA

For information about special discounts for bulk purchases, please contact Sunbury Press Orders Dept. at (855) 338-8359 or orders@sunburypress.com.

To request one of our authors for speaking engagements or book signings, please contact Sunbury Press Publicity Dept. at publicity@sunburypress.com.

FIRST MILFORD HOUSE PRESS EDITION: August 2020

Set in Adobe Garamond | Interior design by Crystal Devine | Cover design by Terry Kennedy | Edited by Lawrence Knorr.

Publisher's Cataloging-in-Publication Data
Names: Wilbur, Doris, author.
Title: A lenape captive : ahmeya / Doris Wilbur.
Description: First trade paperback edition. | Mechanicsburg, PA : Milford House Press, 2020.
Summary: A native woman and her small daughter must learn how to survive alone in a vast forest or become prey to the animals and men who want to harm them.
Identifiers: ISBN : 1-978-620063-25-5 (softcover).
Subjects: FICTION / Historical | FICTION / Native American & Aboriginal | FICTION / Women.

Product of the United States of America
0 1 1 2 3 5 8 13 21 34 55

Continue the Enlightenment!

DEDICATED TO

the Eastern Native Americans
whose culture, arts, spirituality, and
great respect for nature
has much to teach us.

CHAPTER 1

The late 1700s, in the wilderness by Seneca Lake, New York.

AHMEYA RUSHED AWAY WITH KUSKUSKY ON her back, constantly checking behind her as she headed towards the northern point of the vast lake. Although her daughter could walk, Ahmeya could get away much faster by carrying her. Scenes of the horrific battle she just witnessed between the colonial soldiers and her beloved Lenape family kept flashing before her eyes. Blinking hard, she struggled to shut out the gruesome visions of Tamataunee, her Seneca husband, and Mahonoy, her Lenape mother, dying. She forced herself to concentrate, shaking her head, *no, do not think of that now, run away from here, distance yourself far from the killing and the killers. But are we being followed?* She checked behind her, then looked forward through her tear-filled eyes into the woods, seeking a passage between the dense trees that forested the mountainside above Seneca Lake. *There is an opening, go through there, run past those trees, keep going, hurry, do not stop.*

Ahmeya hoped to find another Seneca village where there would be others like her and help, so she followed the contour of the lake's shoreline. Now, working higher with each step, they were halfway up the mountain that cradled the wide sparkling lake. Hours passed, and she no longer heard sounds of the battle or breathed the acrid smoke

1

of her village and crops burning. She was alone right now, but could someone be pursuing them? Her eyes kept searching for a pathway that might lead back down to another Seneca village. She would tell them what took place and seek refuge now that her home had been destroyed.

Almost giving up, she happened upon a well-worn trail heading down the mountainside and into the basin of the valley where the deep lake lay. Ahmeya followed it for a distance as it descended steeply and soon glimpsed a cluster of wooden structures. Peering closer at the buildings below, she watched the activity of Seneca Indians working. That tribe had become friends of the Lenape when they relocated to Seneca Lake. They were picking corn and going about their harvest activities just as her people had been doing. Driving herself even harder to hurry, to get to them, she rushed ahead. She needed to let them know what happened nearby and wanted powerful members of their tribe around her with weapons. A small cliff opening appeared in the woods, and she stepped close to the edge to have a clear view. Her village was out of sight, far in the distance now, but looking closer, she saw columns of black smoke rising straight up into the sky and dust from what must be the advancing march of General Sullivan's force of over 4,000 soldiers. They had completed their brutal carnage and were marching further north to destroy more villages like hers, she realized. Concerned what that might mean, she studied the peaceful scene in the unfamiliar Seneca village.

"We would not be safe down there, Kuskusky," she told her daughter. Then, silently to herself, she thought. *The soldiers will be here soon to kill and destroy as they did in our village, and we might be caught by them this time.*

Ahmeya stood motionless, overlooking the village, struggling with the urge to go on down and warn them. But that would cause her to lose time distancing herself from the line of soldiers snaking its way towards them now.

These Seneca would insist I stay, and they will say they can defend themselves against the white soldiers. They do not understand how many and how powerful these cruel men are. Ahmeya froze, torn with inde-cision between warning the village below and wanting to keep run-ning away to save Kuskusky from the horde getting closer. Hearing a commotion, she saw an Indian runner enter the village, shouting and pointing back towards the fires and line of advancing men. Seneca men, women, and children were gathering around the runner as he urged them all to escape. Ahmeya let out a deep sigh. Now they knew. *I can hurry on, keep running away, there will be no sanctuary or safety for us in that village.* The soldiers would enter it and destroy everything soon. How many more Seneca will fall to the same fate? She wondered. Ahmeya turned around, headed back up the trail, and escaped into the deep woods once more.

She dared not stop to rest or let her guard down with the soldiers so close. They may even be scouting in these woods to find more vil-lages for the troops to destroy. *We will be captured, and what would the soldiers do to us?* She did not want to think about that either, having just seen them killing Indian women and children. The gap between her and the soldiers was closing, and she constantly checked around for pursuers or scouts. Her only hope to keep ahead of them was that they would follow General Washington's orders and stop and *'lay waste to everything in Indian country.'* She felt a terrible sadness knowing that the destruction of another Seneca village and its inhabitants would give her more time to get away.

Ahmeya did not want to alarm her daughter but knew they must go forward and run as fast and far away from the soldiers as they could this day. She pushed herself hard until dusk when it became too dif-ficult to pick out a path in front of her. Her legs and back ached, her heart was heavy with loss, and her mind throbbed with worry and fear. Darkness crept into the forest as the western sun at Ahmeya's back started to bury its face under the green covers of the distant mountains. Ahmeya needed to find a place for the night. It was impossible to see more than a few feet ahead. Trying to travel further in the dark would be useless and dangerous. She could walk off a cliff, twist an ankle by stepping in a hole or become prey for the animals that hunted in the dark. The late August air was still warm, so she and Kuskusky would be okay without furs to cover them as they usually had in the longhouse of Mahonoy.

Pangs of sorrow hit her when she thought of her Indian mother, Mahonoy. The gentle Lenape mother had adopted her so many years ago after her capture from her parent's cabin near Teaoga, Pennsylvania, by the Susquehanna River. Two Lenape Indians had broken into their cabin at the break of dawn one day and taken her mother Ina, and her brothers Rubin and Christopher, along with Ahmeya. She was separated from them and taken on a grueling trek walking over mountains and crossing frigid streams to the River of Pines many miles away. It happened when she was a young colonial girl, only nine years old. When she arrived at the Great Meadows by the River of Pines, an older Indian woman, Mahonoy, adopted her and raised Ahmeya as her own Lenape daughter.

Just that morning, her Indian mother had been murdered by the soldiers. And Tamataunee, her brave Seneca husband, had tried to protect Mahonoy from harm but was unable to save her or himself. He was cruelly struck down also. *Kuskusky and I would have been murdered too if we had not been off high into the woods gathering herbs and roots.* She shuddered at the overwhelming loss of her husband and Indian mother; *I could not even bury them properly, with furs and pots of food to use in the afterlife.* Her eyes almost spilled over, yet she did not shed tears or become overwhelmed. She must stay alert, be strong, and focus on protecting her daughter. Ahmeya knew the spirits of Tamataunee and Mahonoy still walked the earth even though their bodies lay lifeless, and they would walk it for eleven more days. I must save my mourning for later. Now, we must survive.

The darkness of the strange woods became thick and folded like a fur around her. The close forest felt as if they were in a black cave. She must stop and rest. Kuskusky had already fallen asleep while being carried when Ahmeya saw a group of towering pine trees that could be a shelter. One unusually large one had broad limbs that drooped down and touched the earth. Carefully she pushed back a limb and peered inside to make sure no animal hid beneath the thick pine boughs. It was safe, so she moved the limb aside to get underneath and be near the trunk. The area beneath the canopy was small, and she broke off some dead protruding branches to make more room. It became like a small low teepee with a lodgepole trunk and drooping limbs as walls.

Snapping off another long, dead branch, she noticed its sharp pointed end and kept it within reach. It might serve as a spear if needed to defend them. Kuskusky was sound asleep now, and Ahmeya carefully slid her from her back and settled her onto the bed of brown pine needles and green moss built up like a soft cushion around the base of the old tree. Now they were well hidden under the branches that were heavily laden with long pine needles. Only a few little patches of twilight peeked through small openings between the limbs above her. The air smelled of Brother Pine, a familiar, comforting scent. Gazing into the branches high above, she noticed a pair of small brown birds snuggled together roosting for the night.

"This is a safe place for us to sleep, Kuskusky," she said, cuddling her close, "and we will be warm enough too." Ahmeya took a deep, ragged breath and then let it out slowly, thinking about their immediate situation. Brother Pine shut out the rest of the world for the moment and made her feel somewhat safe, but other animals hungry for food roamed the night in these strange woods and probably Colonial soldiers as well.

A rustling sound suddenly got her attention, and she reached for the makeshift spear lying close to her. Gripping it tightly and holding her breath, she listened intently but did not hear anything except the regular breathing of her small daughter and her own pounding heart. After a few minutes, she loosened her grip on the stick and relaxed. Then she heard an animal much closer and grabbed her spear again. Every one of her senses was alert, and her skin crawled with fear. It could be any of the wild animals that hunted at night, a mountain lion, a wolf, she did not know. Carefully she moved a branch back just enough to peek out, fearing what she might see. It was only a big raccoon making all the noise digging in the leaf matter for grubs. Relieved, she exhaled slowly and leaned back.

Ahmeya was on edge and drained physically and emotionally with worry about Kuskusky and the loss of her Indian family. She had pushed herself to exhaustion that day and traveled far while carrying Kuskusky. Her physical aches were nothing compared to the tremendous pain in her broken heart. *Mahonoy and Tamataunee are gone, gone forever. How can I live without them?*

When Ahmeya took stock of what she carried with her, she only had a few pieces of dried meat that would not last long, and greens gathered earlier when she first went into the woods. She had no extra clothing and no tools or weapons except the knife she used for gathering herbs and now a feeble spear-like broken limb. *How will we survive if I cannot find another Seneca village safe from the soldiers?* This part of the mountains or what lay beyond them was unknown to her. Ahmeya reached up and took the precious white comb out of her hair that Tamataunee had carved from an antler so long ago. Staring at the silhouette of the deer, she remembered the love shining in his eyes when he gave it to her. She clutched it to her heart, hoping it would ease the knifing pain piercing her there.

Where should she go now? What should she do? Her village was gone and other villages near it. She knew of no other place to go for help. Then a conversation she had with Tamataunee came back to her. Her brave had told her about a great meeting place of the Iroquois Confederacy somewhere to the northeast of Seneca Lake. They were the keepers of the Council Fire and ruled over all the tribes. Some dignitaries had traveled down from there to visit Mahonoy's village. The Iroquois came to tell the Lenape a treaty had been made with the white chief in Washington, and they must move from the River of Pines and go north or west to live. Mahonoy, Ahmeya, and some others from their village decided to move north and settled by Seneca Lake, and that was where she met Tamataunee, a Seneca brave.

He had told her the Iroquois Council Meeting Place, the seat of government for the six nations, was by a lake the Creator had made touching the earth with his fingers, and many Iroquois lived there. Would she be able to find that place on her own? Surely, they would not turn a woman and child away. Many Iroquois meant safety and help for her. Ahmeya fell asleep thinking of that distant meeting place. Sometime during the night, Ahmeya felt Tamataunee's presence beside her and heard him whisper, *"I walk with you."* But when she reached out for him, she only felt cold earth under her hand.

Ahmeya woke when Kuskusky started stirring next to her. Abruptly sitting up, she saw bright daylight and remembered where they were. *I must begin walking north again right now.* She stood, straightened her clothing, and helped Kuskusky to her feet. She moved a branch of the pine tree aside and peeked out. The woods were alive with blue jays calling and flitting around from trees and bushes, and grey squirrels stirred leaves on the ground as they chased each other. Seeing no signs of danger, they stepped out into the early morning sunshine. She started to walk away from the tree, then returned to get the sharp stick she had broken off last evening. Right now, it would be her walking stick, but it may become a weapon to defend herself and her child.

Walking quickly away, she headed northeast, with her back to where Seneca Lake lay in the basin between the mountains. "We are taking a long walk again today, Kuskusky, and are looking for a good path." Something felt right about this way; perhaps the Ancestors were guiding her. Stressed and alone in the strange woods with her daughter, she remembered something Tamataunee told her one day when he was going off into the woods by himself. He seldom hunted with anyone else and preferred to go after big game, even bear, alone. She worried about him getting hurt and asked him. "Aren't you afraid something will happen, you could take a bad fall and get a broken bone, or perhaps a mountain lion might attack you when no one is there to help you?"

He replied, "I am never alone, even when I am at my weakest. My powerful Ancestors are within me, their blood, their knowledge, their strength is always there for me." He seemed to have no fear of anything bad happening because of his belief.

That day she told him, "And I am here too, Tamataunee, know that I will always be waiting for you to come back from hunting to my arms." They held each other tenderly close for several moments before he left that day. He did return as promised and brought venison for them and other members of the tribe. Now he was gone, and she felt an emptiness in her soul. *He will never return to my arms again except in the afterlife.*

Ahmeya shut that thought out of her head. She must keep her thinking clear so she could plan how to keep her and Kuskusky alive. Mentally she kept going over their needs, thinking about how they could survive in the woods. Kuskusky understood little of what Ahmeya said as they walked. In Kuskusky's mind, they would return to the village soon, and she would be back in the familiar longhouse of Mahonoy. She had no understanding of how her young life had changed forever. That was a blessing.

"We will need shelter each night, Kuskusky. We can make a lean-to, that is something I know how to do, and you can help me." Tamataunee had shown Ahmeya how to build one with limbs and pine boughs, leaves, and bark for a roof. "We will also need food and water every day too." She was so grateful Mahonoy had adopted her in the Lenape village at the River of Pines. Some Indians treated their captives as slaves and worked them hard, never showing them any compassion. Mahonoy was not like that, and the old squaw had been very kind to her. Mahonoy was revered as the herbalist for the Lenape, a Nentpikes. Ahmeya learned all about healing and edible plants, berries, roots, and nuts in the woods and meadows from Mahonoy. Ahmeya smiled, remembering a day in the woods so long ago when she got all turned around, gathering herbs and got separated from Mahonoy.

When she started walking the wrong way, Mahonoy caught up to her. "You look like a rabbit running round and round who forgot where his burrow home was." She took Ahmeya's hand and gently pointed in the direction that led back to their Lenape village. After that, Mahonoy spent time teaching her how to tell east from west and north from south, and Ahmeya became sure of which direction she traveled when in the woods. Ahmeya was not so sure now and hoped she had chosen the right direction. She wished so much that Mahonoy would take her hand once again.

Ahmeya continued to walk in a diagonal direction up to the top of the steep forested mountain. Her thought was if she got high enough, she might be able to look over the land around her and perhaps spot the large lake where the Iroquois council place should be. That would be assurance they were walking in the right direction to reach it. Climbing up to the summit, she kept searching for familiar food that might be growing around them. They had not eaten in some time, and hunger pangs were reminding her to eat; Kuskusky must be hungry as well. *We must eat and stay strong; we have a long way to go.* Berries and nuts were plentiful in late August, and where sunlight pierced the woods, it was lush with edible green plants. Ahmeya had worn her large deerskin carrying bag yesterday when entering the woods, and now she saved wood sorrel, wild mushrooms, and beech nuts in it. When she came across some dogbane, she kept some leaves and fibers from its stem. It was valuable as a protective charm, and she hoped it would keep them from harm. She stopped just for a moment when she saw the dark, speckled bark of a sweet birch tree and peeled some off for making tea but did not linger long. They had to keep moving. Sometimes Ahmeya played a game with Kuskusky and told her to "Run ahead to that white birch tree and stop." Then when Ahmeya reached her, she would tickle her and say, "Now, run to that fat old log and stop." The game kept Kuskusky always moving forward and made walking more bearable.

However, they would not be safe until she was miles away from those terrible soldiers. Then thinking about their provisions, she asked Kuskusky, "What am I going to do without our corn, my daughter?"

"Our corn?" Kuskusky replied, then not understanding what was happening she said: "We will pick some."

Ahmeya thought about all the effort the whole village put into growing their corn. When spring came, the women dug holes in the moist brown earth with tools the men made from the shoulder blades of a deer. They mounded dirt up, placed a fish into each hill, added corn, bean, and squash seeds they had saved from last year's harvest, and carefully covered it all. They nurtured their crops by carrying water all during the growing season when needed. The chasquem grew tall, and the beans used the stalks as a support for climbing. The large squash leaves shaded the roots of both and helped keep them from drying out.

The children stood watch on platforms and whooped and hollered and swung leather cords with rocks on the end over their heads to scare the birds, deer, raccoons, and possums away when the cornstalks were large enough to bear their silky ears of corn. Finally, the corn silk became dark brown, and the fat ears were pushing on their faded wrappings and bending outward from the stalks. It was the time of the Corn Harvest.

The whole village helped pick the corn, husk it, dry it, and put much of it in large baskets before the soldiers came. Many Lenape and Seneca were busy with that chore when the soldiers stormed into the village, firing their weapons, and brandishing their swords. Now, all that growing and harvesting work had been in vain because the soldiers burned and destroyed everything following General Washington's orders. Even the trees in their apple, cherry, peach, and pear orchards were girdled all around their base so they would die and never be fruitful again. Fields and food stores had been destroyed or plundered for the army's use. "Our beautiful corn," Ahmeya said sadly, "we will have to live without our corn Kuskusky."

The sound of a woodpecker drumming loudly on a tree echoed in the forest, and Ahmeya motioned to Kuskusky to be quiet. When they crept closer to the bird, they saw it was as large and black as a crow and had a bright scarlet head with white patterns on its black feathers. They were able to get close to it because the bird had been so busy chipping away and prying off pieces of wood to get at grubs. He was making a sizeable oval-shaped hole in the old dead maple. Chunky yellowish wood chips were piling up at the base of the tree as he angled his head left and right while his big sharp beak chiseled away. "Perhaps he is making a new home, that is what we need." Alarmed by her voice, the large bird stared at them, then spread his mighty wings and flew off, weaving his way between the trees.

They continued to walk deeper into the woods. In some areas, Ahmeya and Kuskusky saw piles of gnawed pinecones lying around the bases of pine trees. Squirrels had chewed the seeds from the cones and left behind thin, brown, corncob middles. Another time, the booming noise of a startled partridge burst into flight from its resting place under a bush. It made them both jump and then laugh when they realized what it was.

At times she carried Kuskusky on her back, and others led her by the hand. Ahmeya kept walking higher until she neared the top of the mountain where it became level. Her thoughts turned again to Tamataunee and the terrible sadness of his loss weighing so heavy on her heart. The Lenape believed that his soul still walked the earth for several days. "Are you here with me today, my love?" Peering into the surrounding forest, she listened and watched carefully for a sign, but no answer came. Forcing her mind to get back to what must be done right now to survive, she focused on what was in front of her, planning their next steps forward.

When they finally reached the summit, heavily foliaged trees stood thick together and made it impossible to see off into the distance. "I will have to climb one of these trees, Kuskusky." She noticed a tall, massive old oak that rose above the other trees. It had thick, muscular looking limbs that would make a good climbing tree with strong branches to support her. She told Kuskusky to stay right there at the base of the tree, Momma, Àna will be right back down. Climbing was difficult at first. Ahmeya had not climbed a tree since being a teenager, but she managed to get high up in it, and before long, she was able to look over the treetops.

Hugging the trunk close, she was able to see the vista surrounding her in all directions. To the west, the waters of the big Seneca Lake still sparkled. The waters were peaceful as if nothing happened there, but more devastation had taken place along its banks because there were still black clouds billowing up into the sky from fires where several villages were burning. So many, many fires, she thought. She glimpsed several soldiers' campfires along the banks also. *They must be resting now but will still be advancing to destroy more villages deep into Seneca country. I was wise to leave there. I hope many Seneca have escaped.* But in her heart, she knew many would stay and fight. They would be defeated by the sheer numbers of the enemy and the weapons used against them.

Far away to the south was the land of the Lenape. Her tribe had been forced to leave there because the settlers pushed them out. A new treaty had given their land away. Northern Pennsylvania was out of sight except in her mind's eye, but she remembered her peaceful life in her Lenape village by the River of Pines. She scanned the direction where she hoped the Great Council Fire of the Iroquois was. Tamataunee told her about the Cayuga, who lived there, a tribe of the Iroquois Confederacy. Ahmeya strained to see into the distance. Far, far away past some more wooded mountains, a distant lake lay in the basin of a valley reflecting the light of the sky. *That is where I need to go; I will find help and shelter in that direction. I will set my path towards the Cayuga, who will help me. Until then, Kuskusky and I must survive and will keep walking until we reach the place of the Great Council Fire.* Ahmeya looked down towards the base of the tree. Kuskusky was supposed to be playing there, but all she saw was a pile of pinecones. Suddenly worried, she called out her name and started quickly descending the tree.

"Kuskusky, where are you?" There was no answer, again she called out her name while descending, "Kuskusky, come here." Her daughter was young, how far could a little girl wander away? Ahmeya wondered. *Was I up in that tree lost in thought too long?* Near the bottom, she jumped to the ground and called out Kuskusky's name repeatedly. The only answer was the echo of her calls. She stopped and listened intently for any sound. Then Ahmeya heard a movement and noise just past some bushes. It sounded like Kuskusky quietly laughing. Quickly running in that direction, she was relieved at finding her little daughter until she saw the reason for her laughter, a Kawiya. Kuskusky was headed towards a porcupine that was oblivious to anyone's presence as it dug under a rotted log. Kuskusky had no idea the danger the porcupine posed to her and continued to reach out to touch it. "Do not touch it, stay where you are!" Ahmeya shouted to Kuskusky, who was so close to it now. She rushed to scoop her up away from the dangerous porcupine. Its quills would blind Kuskusky if they struck her eyes, and if it swung its tail around to strike out at her dozens of barbs would penetrate her delicate skin and stay there, causing great pain. The sharp barbs would have to be pulled out backward one at a time. A painful thing to do, especially for a small child, and it caused a lot of bleeding. If they got broken off, the barbs could even migrate further into her little body, even into her heart or other organs.

Alarmed, Ahmeya reached her just in time and pulled her back. Kuskusky was so close to it. The porcupine became startled from the commotion, swung around, and faced them, snarling. All its quills had been flattened against its body but now were raised straight out, armed, and ready to do harm. It made angry warning noises at them and would undoubtedly lash out if they came closer. Ahmeya knew it could not throw those barbs, only whip its tail out to strike them with it, but it was still terribly dangerous. "Go away, leave us now; we mean no harm." She spoke firmly to the porcupine as she backed Kuskusky up and kept her eyes on it while urging Kuskusky to be quiet. Finally, the animal relaxed its quills slightly, turned, and ambled off in the opposite direction. Relieved, Ahmeya hugged Kuskusky tight and kissed her cheek. "That was too close, now we must go for a walk, little one." She took her hand, and they continued to head northeast through the forest.

Once they passed through the more level crest of the mountain, the land started sloping downward again, and walking became easier. Ahmeya found little bits of food to eat along the way. A few dried blueberries here, some hickory nuts in another spot, some wintergreen leaves to chew for their minty taste. It was just small morsels but something. Some of it they stopped for a moment and ate where they found it, others were put into her carry bag to save for a later time. She alternated between having Kuskusky walk and carrying her on her back.

Ahmeya felt her small daughter fall asleep occasionally while carrying her. She would become quiet, and then she felt Kuskusky's weight slump against her. At other times Kuskusky would chatter away as if they were on an adventure. They had walked back down the other side of a mountain and were going through a narrow valley when it started to become dark. "Where shall we rest tonight, Kuskusky?" she asked.

"Momma, go back to Mahonoy, longhouse." That was impossible. Ahmeya was struck again with the sadness of losing her family and home.

"No, Kuskusky, we must keep walking for some days yet." Her beautiful child could never understand or grasp what happened to her.

Darkness fell around them quickly once the sun started to go down. There was an area against a bank with large grey boulders sticking out of it. She gathered some long sticks and propped them against the stones on a slant. Kuskusky picked up some small sticks too and handed them to her, proud of helping with the task they were doing. Ahmeya then broke off some leafy limbs from sapling trees nearby and lay them on the slanted sticks for a covering on their lean-to. Satisfied she had created a shelter, she told Kuskusky to go inside and sat down beside her. Ahmeya reached into her carry bag for food to share with her and pulled out the remaining dried pieces of meat and a few greens.

They had sipped cold water a short while earlier before stopping to rest that helped fill up their stomachs. The night was warm, so once again, they would be okay without furs to cover them. Ahmeya was thankful for the warm weather but knew it would not last much longer. The time of the corn harvest was over, and cold nights would be coming soon. Holding a tired Kuskusky close, she told her about the Little Braves who live in the forest and protect them. Before long, Kuskusky fell asleep. When she looked down at her innocent child's face, Ahmeya worried about how to keep her safe and what dangers there may be ahead of them. Before the massacre, she had a daily routine, and she had certainties in her life on which she could depend. Now, she had no idea what challenges she might face tomorrow or in the days after that. "How can I protect you, little one?" she whispered.

Ahmeya remembered the time Tamataunee first told her about the small forest braves. The longhouse fire lighted his smiling face as he told the story to her and Mahonoy. They were all so happy that night. "My love, I need you," she said aloud. She still could not weep for his loss or let herself fall apart. Ahmeya took the beautiful white comb out of her hair again and held it in her hand. She admired the intricate carving he had done with just his knife and remembered his shyness when he gave it to her on their second meeting. Kuskusky's straight black hair and dark skin reminded her so much of Tamataunee. Ahmeya gazed at the brilliant stars in the cloudless night sky. She knew they were her Lenape and Seneca Ancestors watching over her and felt comforted by their presence. Soon Tamataunee and Mahonoy's spirits would stop walking the earth and join them in the Land of the Ancestors within a few days. She could not say his name out loud any longer. Once someone died, their name passed with them and was never spoken again. "I miss you, my love," were her last words before falling asleep.

CHAPTER 2

ORNING ARRIVED, AND IT WAS GOING to be warm and sunny. They moved to a stream near-by, and Ahmeya washed and cleaned Kuskusky's face and hands. Both the Lenape and Seneca believed that regular washing was imperative to keep bad spirits away. Soon they continued walk-ing. Curious chickadees with black-capped heads flitted among the trees and bushes and sang chicka-dee-dee-dee around them. When they came to a more open meadow, the white disks of Queen Anne's Lace, fuzzy pink blooms of Joe Pye Weed, and mustard yellow stems of Goldenrod grew everywhere, attracting butterflies and bees to come and get nectar from them. Ahmeya decided her objec-tive was to find safety in the home of the Great Council Fire, and she would walk until she reached it. She was confident there would be many Indians there, and she could get help, shelter, and protection for her and her daughter.

Once she got closer to that place, she would probably find a well-worn path that would lead her right to its location. It was the focus of authority for the tribes and where the Indians got their salt. Briny water from a spring was evaporated into salt crystals there. Hunters and travelers often carved symbols and maps into the smooth bark of trees as trail guides to find the way to shelters, good hunting, or other villages. They would also leave warnings about places overrun by bears or other dangers. Perhaps there were marks left behind on a tree to help guide her. Ahmeya watched for images on the big beech trees around her, but she had not seen any yet. The valley they walked through ended, and she was forced to go up the side of another mountain.

Kuskusky hugged her mother tightly around her neck as she started climbing upward through the trees. They came across a cluster of walnut trees and stopped to pick up handfuls of green, husk covered nuts. It was a real find because they held a lot of nourishment for them both. The large nuts were extremely tough to break open and handling them often stained hands and fingers dark brown. As Ahmeya picked some up, angry red squirrels ran away and scolded the intruders with loud clucking noises and shakes of their tails for plundering their winter bounty. Ahmeya eyed them wishing she had a bow and arrow, but the meat would require cooking. She thought she could create fire after watching how Tamataunee had gotten tinder burning more than once, but there was no time to make a fire now, and soldiers could see the smoke. She had to keep moving.

Ahmeya went higher and higher on the mountainside. They happened upon a big stand of Hemlock trees. Their limbs bore short, fine needles laden with hundreds of tiny cones, and many had fallen to the ground. As Ahmeya and Kuskusky moved forward, a massive flock of turkeys they had disturbed engulfed them. The large dark birds were running, launching into the air, flying and whirling all around them in a mass of confusion. The explosion of beating wings and squawking noise while they escaped was deafening. The enormous swirling flock of heavy birds was so dense it blocked out the light and the forest. Shielding Kuskusky against her, Ahmeya put her head down and covered her face fearing one might collide with them. It was over in just minutes but seemed to take longer as they stood still and held their breath. After the last birds were gone, the woods were silent again, only dislodged feathers and dust was left behind floating to the ground. Kuskusky looked up at Ahmeya with her mouth open and eyes wide unsure of what had just happened. Ahmeya was astounded at seeing such an enormous flock of turkeys let alone being in the middle of hundreds.

When Ahmeya reached the top, there was an open space allowing her to see the region beyond them to the north. The distant lake she had spotted a glimpse of, appeared even further away now. She would have to walk up and down several of the rounded mountains to get there for sure. She scanned the landscape but could not see any settlements or wisps of smoke from any Indian camps anywhere. It was only more dense timber and rows of rounded green mountains and valleys with small streams winding along the bottomlands. "I pray the Ancestors are helping us find the way," she told Kuskusky. Secretly she had a gnawing fear she would never find another Lenape, Seneca, or other Indian settlement.

What if I do not? She wondered. *How can I take care of my child, make our shelter, get food, and defend ourselves from animals who wish to do us harm?* "I do not know what to do. I need you, my love," she spoke aloud to the spirit of Tamataunee. Fatigue, discouragement, and lack of proper food were setting in, and she felt completely overwhelmed with mourning and so alone. She studied the rows of ancient green mountains and valleys that stretched ahead of them yet. Then she saw an all-white deer appear from the pines in the valley below her. It stood out starkly from its emerald surroundings. The white deer browsed for a few minutes, then turned around and disappeared back into the forest. In a moment, it was gone. She had heard about the ghost deer of the Seneca from several hunters who had seen a white deer and talked about it. They never tried to kill one. They considered them sacred. Tamataunee had told her of the white deer when he carved one on her hair comb.

Suddenly realizing this may be a sign from Tamataunee, she wondered, *had he heard her plea? Was the white deer showing her the direction to go? This might be his answer.* Ahmeya descended the mountain and walked into the valley where the white deer had been. There was no sign of it now, yet she felt sure she was meant to follow its lead. "Show me the way, my love," she asked of her dead husband's spirit, "show me the way." She walked with Kuskusky along the border of a winding stream. Following its course, she soon came across a beaver dam with a sizable pool of water behind it. There was a large domed shaped beaver lodge composed of piled up sticks and mud back along one edge of the pond. Ahmeya was so fatigued from days of walking up and down mountainsides, and now she did not know which direction to go. Feelings of desperation came back and were testing her resolve. *I am just going to roam these woods forever,* she thought, *until we freeze in winter or hungry animals get us. Maybe I should stop here. We would have water for drinking, and I could build a shelter and get food. There must be fish here to catch, and I could make a snare to capture game. I am so tired.* Grief and fatigue were catching up to her. It was getting much harder to keep pushing herself and not give up.

Ahmeya found a place beneath shady trees where she and Kuskusky could rest and watch the beaver at work. Nearby was a stump of an aspen tree the tëakwe had chewed until it fell, and he stripped it of its branches to haul away for food, or to repair its lodge or dam. Ahmeya picked up a big chip of wood the beaver had chewed. She turned it over and over in her hands, looking at the teeth marks on the big chip as she watched the large rodent swimming. How could a beaver cut down such a big tree with just its teeth? She felt the hardness of the wood in her hands and examined the tall, grey barked aspen trees the beaver was harvesting. Out of curiosity, she put the wood chip into her mouth and bit down to see how hard it was, and her teeth did not even dent the wood. Then she saw Kuskusky pick up a chip and put it in her mouth and bite on it too. Laughing she told her no, it was not food for people, just the beaver. Kuskusky took the chip out of her mouth, made a funny face while sticking her tongue out, and threw the chip into the water.

Ahmeya thought it was such an impossible task to gnaw through the base of these big trees with just his teeth to make them fall. Yet, the beaver does it because that is what he must undertake to live. She studied the solid dam he had built to hold back the stream. It had caused the water to back up and produced a large, deep pond. His big dome-shaped lodge for getting dry and sleeping was sticking above the water. It was made of sticks he had gnawed into just the proper lengths for building his lodge and mud, and then he added mud and grasses to complete the structure. There was a raised platform inside where the family could rest and get dry. It was constructed well enough for him to live with his family through the bleakest of winters, and he had a submerged entrance so he could go into the pond even when it was frozen solid. She sat silently for several moments and then decided *I cannot give up now. If that small animal can build all this with no tools, I should be able to take care of Kuskusky and myself until we reach the Cayuga. I must walk on to their country. I have got to find the Council Meeting Place.*

An eagle circled above them and landed on the skeleton of an old dead tree sticking out of the water. It peered at Ahmeya then swung its head back and forth while scanning the water's glassy surface for movement. Suddenly it opened its broad wings, and with eyes fixated on its target, it swooped down with a splash and plucked a fish from beneath the water. It sailed off with the fish gripped in its talons facing forward. The eagle had flown off in the same direction the white deer had gone, and she recognized the exact spot where the white deer had disappeared into the woods earlier. *It is another sign, that is the way I must set my path.* She stood up, took Kuskusky's hand, and started walking into the forest opening.

They walked on, and she worked her way through dense stands of pines, hemlocks, and clusters of sugar maples, beech, birch, and basswood trees. Many trees were so massive their canopies blocked out the sun and formed an expansive roof over her and Kuskusky. Pointing to an unusually large beech, she told Kuskusky, "We could live in that tree like a possum and hang upside down from the limbs."

Kuskusky thought that was funny and giggled, "You will be possum momma, and I will be possum baby." They laughed about that and talked of the different kinds of forest homes they could make as they walked on. They could live in a cave, like a bear, or tunnel into the ground like a rabbit and so on. Ahmeya traveled through damp gullies where moisture dripped from grey shale ledges and ferns hung heavy from overhangs or carpeted the forest floor they crossed. The soft fronds caressed their legs as they walked among them. Small streams and little waterfalls talked to her with their musical melodies of water flowing and falling on step-like stones, urging her to stop, rest, and listen to them, but she continued walking on, carrying Kuskusky when her little legs became tired. Ahmeya tried to stay positive and not let her mind go to the dark, discouraging place it had been earlier. *I will discover a path or a marking left by a hunter who traveled this way. If I can find a big river or stream large enough for a canoe to travel, it would probably lead to the Cayuga. I will follow that northeast.* However, all around were just mountains, dense woods, marshes, and gullies. They walked on, and more days passed without detecting any marks left on trees or finding streams large enough for a canoe to travel.

They were walking through an open area, and Ahmeya noticed the golden-brown coats of a doe and her fawn eating fruit laying on the ground under a wild apple tree. The fawn had no spots and was almost the size of its mother. They both appeared to be strong and healthy. Ahmeya watched the two browsing beneath the tree as Kuskusky dozed on her back. They pushed their muzzles through the grass and seized an apple before chewing and swallowing it all, including the core. She could hear the loud crunching sound as they bit down on the wild fruit. This large animal survives winter with no shelter and little food, she thought. They do not hibernate, they do not have food stores, and they are out in the weather night and day, summer, or winter. Ahmeya had helped tan deer hides to create garments and was familiar with the hollow hair deer have. It served as insulation to keep them warm even when snow was swirling around them and falling as a cold white blanket on their backs. The big animals were created to survive in the woods and meadows with large ears to hear danger and sharp hooves to walk in snow. They could dig into the earth for food and have sure footing when they suddenly needed to sprint away.

But how could achtu possibly survive winter when every edible green was dead or submerged under the snow, and there were no apples to eat? She wondered. She had seen deer at the end of winter that were so emaciated and weak from starvation they could hardly walk. For several months all they had to browse on was leaf buds and twigs. She realized they must eat everything they can before the snow becomes deep, and all the greens, acorns, and fruit are gone. Thinking of her own situation, she realized they needed more food. Ahmeya walked closer to the apple tree. The startled pair raised their heads and stared at her. Then the doe became alarmed, stamped her foot, and they both bounded away with their white flag tails raised high and waving. She told Kuskusky as she put her down. "Wake up, little one; we have apples to eat." Ahmeya bit into the tart apple flesh and juice dribbled from the corner of her mouth. "Kuskusky, eat some apples, eat all you can," she told her as she handed her a ripe apple. Looking at the apple she had just bitten, she noticed the tunnel of an insect. Then she spotted the tiny crawling worm. Shrugging her shoulders and continuing, she ate the whole apple and only rejected the core.

That night as darkness started to overtake them, she and Kuskusky sheltered with their backs against the overhang of a rocky cliff hidden behind ferns taller than she was. The night was chilly, and she held Kuskusky close, keeping her warm. It had been days now since the massacre back at the shore of Seneca Lake. It was the time when Tamataunee and Mahonoy's spirits would ascend to the land of their Ancestors in the sky. She had felt their presence still with her at moments during the last few days. Now in the black, coldness of the night, she felt a deep, heavy emptiness and sensed they had departed.

Tremendous, agonizing grief filled her heart to bursting. She could not breathe and cried out with great wailing sounds as she yanked out her hair. "They are gone . . . they are gone. They walk the earth no more. I will never touch their flesh again or look into their eyes." She wept long and hard, yet it did not wake an extremely tired Kuskusky. Her deep, sad wailing echoed through the forest, which stilled, tuning in to her heartbroken sobs. Ahmeya cried not solely for the loss of Tamataunee and Mahonoy but for her father Cornelius, too, whom she had recognized as a soldier taking part in the massacre. She grieved for the loss of the Lenape and Seneca and the joyous life she had known in her village. She sobbed for Kuskusky, who would never experience the longhouse of her people or listen to the wisdom of her elders and hear the ancient stories. She shed tears for the skills her child would never learn at the knees of the elders in her village. She cried for the hatred and cruelty men carried in their hearts for others they did not know or even wish to understand. She wept. Heartbroken and alone.

The rain started falling as if the Ancestors had heard her anguish and grieved too. She moved Kuskusky, who was still sleeping soundly, back tighter against the rocky overhang to keep her dry. Drained at last, Ahmeya finally fell asleep holding her daughter and the elegant hair comb with the silhouette of the white deer. In her dream, Tamataunee whispered in her ear as he kissed her goodbye. *"I will always be with you . . . right here."* Then he kissed Kuskusky, and his image was gone.

Ahmeya woke to the sun filtering through the trees. In places, the sun lit patches of ferns, and they glowed bright chartreuse green against the dark forest floor. She reached into her carry bag and found the walnuts they had saved. The green husks were splitting and exposing the dark wooden shell of the nut underneath. Hoping they were ripe enough to eat, she pounded them open with a rock to get the large nutmeats out. They were mature, and she gave Kuskusky several to eat. There were also mushrooms and berries she had saved by gently wrapping them in reindeer moss. It was not much, but it was enough to keep her going and put food in Kuskusky's belly. Not long after eating, they left their shelter under the rock ledge and started walking northeast. The day before, Ahmeya had spotted a white birch tree, cut the bark, peeled the many layers apart, and got a pliable piece she could bend. She had formed a cone of birchbark to use for drinking and a small basket to hold what she collected, which hung from a belt around her waist. Some layers of the bark were paper-thin, and she saved pieces for future use. She had talked to the spirit of the tree as she did her work and thanked it for allowing her to use its bark. She wished she had some sacred tobacco to leave on the ground by it as gratitude.

Later that morning, Ahmeya came across a large bed of leeks growing in a gulley. The lilylike leaves were yellowed, and their single stems bore small umbrella seed heads now in late summer, but beneath the surface, there were plump, white, juicy onion-like bulbs. Kuskusky helped her as they used sharpened sticks to pry out as many leek bulbs as they could. The bulbs were not deep beneath the surface, so it was not hard digging in the soft, moist ground where they preferred to grow. The air was ripe with a garlicky smell. "Kuskusky, I can make soup with these," she told her daughter, who had quit digging and was now occupied with marching and waving a fern leaf. "Somehow, I have to get us fire." Ahmeya had a generous supply of leek bulbs before leaving there. She rinsed the soil off them in clear stream water and stored them away in her deerskin carrying pouch. Before the day was over, she had added more gathered food to her supplies. Ahmeya was more determined and focused better after the release of her sorrow the night before, and discovering the leeks lifted her spirits. They both were in great peril in those dense woods alone, but so far, they were surviving, and she was able to find food and get shelter each night for her and Kuskusky.

When darkness started to wrap around them again, she watched for another place safe from the elements. The vast bulk of an ancient dead tree caught her interest, and she stepped closer to inspect it. Checking around the backside and tapping on it produced an empty, hollow sound, and she discovered the inside had rotted out. Looking at the huge stump closer, she noticed there was an opening, and she might be able to squeeze inside. Cautiously she peered in, fearing it might be the home of an animal but found none. She reached in and pulled out handfuls of crumbling, dry, rotted wood from the interior, and made the space much larger. Bark wrapping the outside of the enormous stump was peeling away in large thick sheets, and she pried off a piece big enough to cover the entry hole.

Kuskusky helped her gather an assortment of ferns and pine branches, and they placed them inside the stump to cover the floor. She climbed in with Ahmeya's help, then Ahmeya stepped inside and used the big piece of bark as a door to close off the entrance. "That should keep any animal from joining us tonight, Kuskusky." It was close inside the trunk, but snug and she felt satisfied that it would serve for the night. When she looked above her, however, she could see the dark evening sky full of stars. The top of the stump was completely open.

It was another cool night, and Ahmeya felt a chill as air descended on them from over their heads. They huddled together inside their hollow tree cave to stay warm. "Tomorrow, I must work on getting us fire," she told Kuskusky. "I need to cook, and we need heat to keep the cold away." The forest was full of noises that night, and she heard wolves howling from a distance. It reminded her that the soldiers were not the only ones out for blood. She kept her sharp walking stick close and held onto it tight as she anxiously scrutinized the large opening above her.

A movement inside the darkness to the left of her head made her jump. Something was crawling on the inside wall right by her face, and she strained to identify what it was. When her eyes were focused better, she could tell it was a small orange salamander resting in the dark with them. She relaxed; it was an innocent creature with which to spend the night. She told it, "Thank you, little one, for sharing your home with us." It blinked its small gleaming black eyes then ever so slowly crawled out of sight. Looking at the opening above, she thought about other forest creatures. "Fire will help us keep brother wolf and bear from visiting us too, Kuskusky." Ahmeya stayed awake and vigilant for quite some time. Before long, Kuskusky fell asleep against her; then, she too sank into another exhausted and restless sleep.

Strange dreams came to her during the night. A large black bear tried to get at her and Kuskusky through the opening above them. It was pawing at the wood with its sharp claws and trying to reach them inside the stump. The ghostly figure of Tamataunee was hovering above the dream bear, telling Ahmeya, "It is okay, let him have you," but she was too frightened to let the bear come in and kept struggling in her dream to beat it back with her sharp walking stick. The bear kept growling loudly, gnashing its teeth and clawing at the stump. Then the bear changed to a bear-like figure of a man wearing a bearskin that was still growling and trying to get into the stump with them. She kept jabbing at it hard and pushing it back from her and Kuskusky. All the time, a mist-like apparition of Tamataunee was hovering above them in the blackness and kept repeating, "Let him devour you. It will be better for you," but she kept fighting the bear back. When she woke the next morning, she struggled to make sense of the disturbing dream. Was it a vision meant to deliver a warning message to her, or was it just a dreadful dream born of fear?

The dream bothered her as they were getting ready to leave their tree shelter. Finally, she put it out of her mind and resolved to make a fire when Kuskusky reminded her she was hungry. After they commenced walking forward, she scanned around her for a small flexible limb to use for a fire bow. The Lenape liked wood with a strong, tight grain for that, but it had to be somewhat limber to bend without snapping. Later, she recognized a small hickory tree and took her knife and cut a section of a young limb over a foot long from it. By that time, it was well past midday, and hunger gnawed at her insides again, and Kuskusky was telling her she was hungry too. They halted at a pleasant opening in the woods to rest and have something to eat. While Kuskusky played, Ahmeya carefully cut a long narrow strip from the shoulder strap of her deerskin carrying bag and tugged on it to test its strength. It did not break, and she thought it might serve as a string for the fire bow.

Now, she needed to find a dry chunk of wood that was flat on the top. She managed to find a short piece, but it was round, so she stood the wood on end, used her knife as a wedge, and striking it with a rock, split the wood right down the middle, so it fell apart into two pieces. Next, she carved a small depression into the flat area of one side while talking away to Kuskusky and explaining what she was doing. "I am going to make a bow and fire stick Kuskusky, so we can cook and have warm soup and tea. Won't that be good to have?"

Kuskusky answered, "yes, Momma" loudly then rubbed her stomach and smiled. Ahmeya told Kuskusky to look nearby for sticks to use for the fire, and Kuskusky quickly started making a small pile of twigs. Ahmeya had seen Tamataunee make a fire with a small bow and a straight stick when they had gone into the woods to stay, but she had never tried it herself. Secretly she doubted she could make it work, but she was determined to try.

Once she got the small round depression carved into the base with the tip of her knife, she gathered tinder material for starting a fire. She carved thin slivers from dry wood and added the paper-thin layers of bark she saved from the birch tree. The deer hide string was fastened to one end of the little bow made from the limber hickory wood. She wrapped the string several times around a straight round stick that was a foot long and secured the other end to the bow. Holding the stick upright in the depression, she tried moving the bow back and forth to make the tall round stick spin. Happy it was spinning the stick at least; she laughed and clapped her hands. Now, she had to make it spin fast enough to create hot friction between the bottom of the stick and the depression in the dry wood. Her first efforts at spinning the stick were comical. She forgot to hold the stick down on the top, and she had to duck as it spun upwards towards her face.

Failing to make things work, her frustration was building. Several times the stick jumped out of the round depression and came off the base completely. The stick was not fitting in the base well because it was flat on the end, and the depression was shaped like a bowl, so she carefully carved the bottom of the stick into a curved shape. Kuskusky sat down by her little pile of twigs and watched and waited. The next issue Ahmeya had was that the base kept moving away from her as she pushed on it. So much was going wrong. She was not holding the bow right and could not work it with a smooth sawing motion, just jerky start and stop movements. Instead of it spinning smoothly and steadily, she was getting it hung up repeatedly. She had been working on producing fire for hours now. Kuskusky had fallen asleep by her pile of twigs and was resting peacefully. Ahmeya's hands were blistered and cramping. After more futile attempts, she became irritated, cursed loudly, and flung the whole thing far away from her. The only fire she was making was the burning anger and frustration she felt inside.

Kuskusky woke and seeing Ahmeya just sitting there, got a pouty look on her face, and asked, "Are we going to make soup, Momma?"

Seeing her daughter's sweet face, she knew she could not quit. She had to try again.

Ahmeya took a couple of deep breaths and let them out gradually to calm herself. Then she rounded up all the pieces she needed again. She deepened the round depression the straight stick turned in, secured the flat dead wood so it could not move by bracing it against a rock, and fixated on keeping the stick and bow moving with steady rhythmic push-pull strokes. Finally, it all worked together, and she gave out a whoop of joy when she saw a tiny wisp of smoke coming from the depression. She spun the stick faster and faster and then halted to see if there was a spark glowing. There was a spark, so she put small pieces of the paper-thin birch bark and fine dry grass on it and gave it a gentle puff of breath to make it flame.

She had fire! She quickly dumped the little pile of flaming tinder onto more dry fine tinder and then fed that bit by bit with some of Kuskusky's small twigs and then pieces of wood followed by larger wood until it was powerful enough to have a steady flame and throw off heat. "We have fire Kuskusky, we have fire!" she shouted as she and Kuskusky jumped around, clapped their hands, and danced, singing "hot, hot, hot." Ahmeya was elated. Now she had a fire for heat, cooking, and protection. Several dead limbs were lying around to make a tripod for cooking. The wood snapped and popped as she broke them into the lengths she needed. By wetting a birch bark basket with water, she could hang it right over the fire without it burning. More water was poured into the basket, and she added leeks and mushrooms for their soup. She cut another strip of deerskin off the strap of her carry bag to hang the basket on the tripod and sat back to admire the fire heating their supper.

The smell of the leek and mushroom soup cooking along with the firelight and warmth was so comforting. Ahmeya felt so accomplished and grateful she raised her voice in song and thanked the Ancestors for giving her their knowledge. She felt safer for no animal would come past the fire to harm them if it was burning. "Maybe we will rest here longer," she told Kuskusky. She was tired mentally and physically and needed to get her strength back. "There is water here, and I can find more food. I can make a snare and catch a rabbit or squirrel for us now that I can cook. That meat would taste good." Her young daughter was already starting to drift off. "Stay awake, Kuskusky; we are going to have warm soup." In a short while, Kuskusky smiled as they smacked their lips and sipped the soup right from the birch bark container.

Ahmeya did choose to stay there for at least one more day, possibly more. Kuskusky fell asleep right after her meal, and while she was sleeping, Ahmeya gathered more dry wood to keep the fire going throughout the night. She arranged a place where they could lie down close to the fire to stay safe and warm. When that was done, she sat down, folded her legs, wrapped her arms around them, and rested her chin on her knees. Kuskusky was sleeping snuggled against her as she watched the dancing flames and glowing sparks drift upwards towards the heavens. The woods were even darker now when she looked away from the bright fire, but she felt much safer with it. Kuskusky was resting peacefully, and it was a relief knowing that her daughter was so innocent and just lived in the moment.

"That is what I must do," she said aloud, "not be so saddened by what is gone and lost that I cannot ever get back. I cannot worry about what may take place tomorrow; the sun has not awakened yet. I must be happy and thankful we are here now. We are alive and together. We have some food and water, and we have fire." Ahmeya studied the clusters of bright stars above her and wondered where her loved ones now lived with the Ancestors. A shooting star streaked across the sky and disappeared as she followed its path. *It would be wonderful to talk to the Ancestors from long ago,* she thought, *and someday I will join them.* Thinking of Tamataunee and Mahonoy, she used her knife to carve two starry symbols into the handle of her walking stick. From then on, when she touched those symbols, she would be reminded of the knowledge Tamataunee and Mahonoy had passed on to her for making shelter, getting food, and making a fire.

CHAPTER 3

ANOTHER DAY PASSED, AND ANOTHER, YET Ahmeya stayed in that area. The beaver pond nearby had a stand of cattails growing and she dug some tubers they could eat later. She also peeled the long stems of the marsh plant, and she and Kuskusky ate the fleshy white parts crunching into the mild-flavored pith and savoring it. Walking around more of the pond, she found some swamp milkweed and stripped long fibers off its brown stems. She planned on twisting the fibers into a cord and hoped it would be strong enough to use as a fishing line with a willow stick for a pole. Worms and bugs were easy to find, but she had no hook for any bait. The Lenape and Seneca traded for metal fishing hooks, but she was not able to do that now. She considered using a wooden thorn from an apple tree. The thorns, often over an inch long, were strong and hard. She had used apple thorns for an awl before, but she discarded using one because they were too straight, and the fish would get away.

Later, back at her camp, she remembered the wish token Mahonoy had given her years ago. She wore it in a small leather pouch around her neck. Removing her necklace, she opened the little deerskin pouch decorated with multicolored glass beads and fringe. She lifted the flap and nestled inside was a copper canoe wish token. Mahonoy had made it for Ahmeya with the wish that someday she would have her own canoe and a family. That wish came true when she married Tamataunee and had Kuskusky. She looked at the other tokens that were in the pouch. There was a tiny bow her friend had made, a silver coin with a face on it, and a miniature ear of corn made of clay. She also had a small yellow feather she had found long ago and some blue beads and pieces of purple wampum. They were all cherished, and she remembered getting each one of them. Ahmeya had made tokens too when she was younger and given them away to her Lenape friends.

Now, she needed the precious metal canoe for something else to survive. Using her knife as a chisel, she pried and hammered the canoe flat. Then she freed a thin strip of metal from one side by repeatedly using a rock to strike the sharp blade of her knife against the copper. The soft metal was easy to bend into a hook with a loop at the top. By rubbing one end of the bent metal strip back and forth on a rock, she made a sharp thin point. Then she heated it until the metal glowed and quickly plunged the hook into water. It had hardened, but would it be too brittle and snap in two at the first pressure of a fish?

In the morning, she twisted fibers from the milkweed and made a long fine twine and tied it onto a willow pole. She fastened the hook onto the end and said a prayer to the Ancestors that it would work. Ahmeya walked back to the pond and found a dry place for Kuskusky to sit on a log and play close by. She overturned an old fallen log and caught a brown worm wriggling beneath one for bait. When all was ready, she carefully cast her makeshift fishing line out onto the water and waited. Promptly, the bait sank below the surface, she felt a tug, pulled on the line, and had hooked a fish. Amazed and happy that it had been that easy, she shouted with joy. Ahmeya held the fish up for Kuskusky to see. "Look what the Great Spirits our Ancestors have given us to eat Kuskusky." Unhooking the fish, she ran a stick through its gills and drove the other end into the earth to keep the fish from slipping away. She inspected her copper hook. It had held up without bending, so she found another worm and cast again. It took longer this time before the tug of a second fish, but soon another pulled on her line.

Ahmeya caught several fish of different sizes before she stopped that day. Two of them she cooked by cleaning them and then threading the filets onto a stick and propping them over the fire. When done, they had a smoky, juicy flavor, and tasted delicious. The remaining fish she fileted and hung in the smoke from the fire to dry for later use. Later that afternoon, Ahmeya and Kuskusky returned to the beaver pond. She had seen several long sticks on the beaver lodge near the shore. The water was not deep, and she waded out to the beaver's home. She pulled out a couple of sticks laying on the top and flung them to the shore. These sticks will help me build a strong roof, she realized. When she reached to pull out another stick from the lodge, she saw a sudden movement. A large snake with a thick muscular body and a triangular head slithered off the top of the big lodge and slid down into the water near her. Terrified, she sucked in her breath and stood totally still. The serpent swam away from her, leaving an S-shaped wake behind it. Thankfully she did not get bitten by the swamp rattler with the catlike pupils.*

Her hand had been reaching for a stick right where the snake was resting. The close call frightened her deeply and made her realize the danger she was in daily now. If she had gotten bitten by that snake, she would have died an acutely painful death from the toxic venom, then what would have happened to Kuskusky? She clutched her chest sickened at the thought of Kuskusky's fate if left alone in the forest. She looked around, making sure there were no more snakes. "I must be very careful that I do not get hurt or sick," she said, speaking to the spirit of Tamataunee. "Our little child depends on only me and the Ancestors to take care of her now."

Ahmeya thanked the beaver for letting her take the sticks even though she had not seen him. She needed to use those sticks as poles for a proper lean-to roof. She had no ax, so she was thankful the beaver had cut the limbs into helpful long sections for her use. Her lean-tos were getting better, and this one was the strongest and best one yet when finished with pine boughs and bark for covering the roof and a fire near the front opening for heat, light, and protection. She lined the floor

---

* Massasuaga Rattlesnake. A snake of the marsh and swamps.

with soft mosses and leaves that Kuskusky helped her gather. Ahmeya was deeply grateful for the gifts the Great Spirit Kishelemukong and the Ancestors gave her. That night before falling asleep by the warmth of the fire, she and Kuskusky sang songs of praise and honor to them.

Ahmeya stayed at that campsite for several days. The fish she caught along with the soups she was able to make restored their strength. She also made a simple doll for Kuskusky out of cattail leaves that had a head and arms, bodice, and skirt, but purposely had no face so Kuskusky could give her doll whatever emotion she wished it to have while playing with it. Ahmeya spent a whole day cutting strips of bark from maple and ash trees. The next day she made a large basket to carry more of what she was gathering, catching, and preparing for them.

Ahmeya collected dry, brown tops from cattails by the pond. The cattails were such a useful plant. She could split the brown tops apart and use the soft white fluff as fire tinder or stuff it into their moccasins for warmth. The pollen was good medicine, and she could weave mats to sit on plus make baskets from the leaves and stalks. The roots could be dried and pounded into a flour. Even the green seed heads and pollen were eaten at the correct time of the year. The provisions and supplies she gathered were making survival possible. When she returned to the beaver pond to get water, Ahmeya noticed signs of a rabbit and decided to try making a snare using more twine she made from the milkweed fibers and a few sticks. Tamataunee had taught her how to make snares, and soon she had one set up with a trigger mechanism that caused a bent stick to spring up when the bait was taken and close the snare around an animal's head. She decided to try a piece of peeled cattail stalk to bait the rabbit. That was not what a rabbit usually ate, but the animal might be hungry enough to try it and get caught. A rabbit in the snare would make her happy; a skunk would not.

Returning the next day, she did find a rabbit in the snare. It appeared to have instantly died, and she was thankful for that. She thanked the spirit of the rabbit for becoming their food. That day they had rabbit meat roasted over the campfire. When she skinned it, she saved the fur to make warm moccasins for Kuskusky. Sitting by the fire that night, she gently loosened the bark on a piece of willow. Then she slipped the bark off, cut a channel and notch, and put the bark back on. It made a nice whistle for Kuskusky. She tied a length of twine onto it so Kuskusky could wear it around her neck. Kuskusky started blowing on her new toy right away and made loud whistles and flutelike sounds. She fell asleep holding her little cattail doll and still had the whistle to her mouth.

Ahmeya and Kuskusky kept active during the day, gathering firewood and foraging for greens and anything else edible. Every night when Ahmeya lay down to sleep, she thanked the Great Spirit and the Ancestors for providing so well for her and Kuskusky and for keeping them safe. After a while, she wondered if she should stay where they were and give up trying to reach the Cayuga. *If Kuskusky and I remain alone somewhere in the wilderness like this, I could save her from knowing the cruelty of men like I have seen. I would protect her from that evil, but it would keep her from knowing the great love of men, as well, love like I had with Tamataunee, and love that comes with having children of her own.*

That would be so cruel to Kuskusky, living an empty, lonely life, never knowing others, and what would she do when I left her to live with the Ancestors? As she thought longer about it, she knew the winters were so brutal they could not possibly survive living in the little shelter she had built. Ahmeya was becoming lonely too. She had no one to talk with except Kuskusky and wished to be with others of her own kind. However, she was providing food for them right now; should she risk giving that up by leaving there? *This may be the safest place for us*, she thought. She questioned her situation over and over and wondered what to do next. Ahmeya fell asleep, still not knowing whether she should stay where they were or leave.

When she woke and went down to the beaver pond for water the next morning, fresh tracks littered the soft mud. Examining them closer, she realized they were from máxku, a large, heavy one by the size of the print and the depth its clawed foot had sunk into the mud. The impression was frightening as she examined how big and long the claws were on its padded feet. With her heart racing, she turned quickly and scanned the woods along the shore. Some distance away, she saw the black hulk of a bear entering the darkness of the woods that edged the marshy area. The animal was leaving, and the wind was at her face, so she knew he would not get her scent, but the knowledge of his close presence was frightening. *What if he comes back and finds our camp?* It will probably return tomorrow to drink or cool off in the water. She thought that maybe he was after the fish or beaver living nearby, but suddenly realized he might smell my cooking. That thought made her freeze in place.

She could build a better shelter and find a way to keep them warm here, but she could never fight off that bear or build something to keep him out with the strength it must have. The bear would brutally kill them. That morning right after she saw the bear, Ahmeya made the decision to leave her camp and head northeast again to the Great Council Fire of the Cayuga. She quickly returned to camp and gathered up everything she could carry.

She had accomplished a lot by resting in this place. She made a basket for carrying supplies and had gotten fish, meat, and other wild foods. She now had a way to fish. She left the pole there; it would be easy to make another and wound up the line with the precious copper hook. She packed her fire-making tools and little pouches of foodstuffs and herbs. She had a way to start a fire now with her bow and firestick and felt confident they would not starve soon, but they needed to get good shelter and warm clothing before the weather got bitter cold, and it was the time when the trees rested. She picked up her walking stick and decided to lash her knife to the end of it so she could use it like a spear against the bear. It was ridiculously small compared to a bear's powerful claws and teeth, but it gave her something to try to fight him off if it attacked them.

The last thing she did was take a glowing ember from the fire and wrap it up in lichen and moss. Then she wrapped that with bark and tied it tightly to keep any air from getting at it until she needed it to start another fire. If the ember went cold, she could at least use her fire-starting bow to make more embers. When she finished preparing the ember bundle, she gazed around wistfully at the little camp. She was reluctant to leave but knew with the bear roaming so close by, he would soon find them. She got her bearings, took Kuskusky's hand, and quickly started walking away from the bear's domain through the woods in a northeast direction.

Ahmeya walked all day, only stopping to give Kuskusky something to eat and drink and let her rest her little legs. They stopped at a clearing where they sat on a fallen log. The sun streamed through the canopy and birds sang from leafy treetops. Kuskusky walked around, picking up small sticks and rocks and made little houses with moss-covered roofs that she said were for the frogs and birds. She carried her small cattail doll with her and talked to it as if it was her playmate.

"She is such a beautiful child, my love," Ahmeya said, talking to her dead husband's spirit again as if he sat on the log right next to her. "I will tell her about you and her Lenape grandmother." Then, remembering how they would no longer be with her, she became extremely sad again. She tried to shake that feeling and told herself, *I cannot dwell on what has happened. I must think of our future now. I must stay strong for Kuskusky.* But sadness was washing over her. She needed to do something to remember them, so she unwrapped her knife from the end of her walking stick and went over to a large beech tree nearby. It had a smooth, light grey bark and would make a perfect surface for what she wanted to do. "Brother Tree, remember my loved ones," she said as she carved the clan symbols of a turtle and a beaver into the bark of the old beech tree.

She stepped back and viewed her carving through misty eyes. She chanted a goodbye song to them and thanked the spirit of the tree before she once again got Kuskusky and walked on. That night she found shelter in amongst a thick cluster of pines and built a small fire with the ember she had carried to keep them warm and safe. Her little camp was only a tiny speck of light in the miles and miles of dark forest surrounding them.

The next morning, she and Kuskusky had something to eat and then left the cluster of pines to walk northeast again. She had chosen the direction she should go on pure instinct and the directional knowledge that Mahonoy and Tamataunee had taught her. "Look at the moss on the trees; which side is it growing on? Look at the flow of the streams. Watch the sun as it travels across the sky and the star that lives in the north." She prayed she was reading all those signs correctly. Sooner or later, if she just kept walking, she had to find others, she was sure of that. Whether they would be friendly or her enemies, she did not know. Hopefully, it would be people like herself and not white people whom she was so afraid of now and distrusted intensely. She had seen firsthand how they would treat the Lenape and Seneca and wanted nothing to do with them.

It was past midday, and despite watching carefully, she still had not come across a trail or major waterway to use as a guide leading her to the Cayuga. The woods around them were still. She walked up a little rise and suddenly stopped when she saw what lay ahead. A puzzling scene lay before her, and she tried to comprehend its meaning. She stood rooted where she was and kept Kuskusky from going forward. A broken tree was hung up in the top of another tree, and a large part of its top had sheared off and fallen straight to the ground. She could tell the tree had been chopped at its base with an ax and was not broken off by a strong wind. A sizeable broken part had crashed to the ground. Underneath all that weight was a man pinned from his knees down.

Ahmeya told Kuskusky to wait right where she was while she carefully crept closer to get a better look. The man lay on his back with one of his arms stretched out. Ahmeya saw the handle of a large felling ax in his hand. She heard buzzing flies, and nearby she saw the body of a grey wolf. His head and chest had been bloodied red by the ax, and it was dead.

The man lay still. Ahmeya went nearer and saw his face was smeared with dirt, but noticed he was a white man with long shaggy hair and a full beard. His eyes were closed, and he showed no signs of life. Ahmeya could tell his legs had been badly broken by the awkward twisted angles of his feet and ankles. Ax marks riddled the log where the man had tried to free himself from the heavy wood pinning him but failed. The wolf must have seen him helpless and tried to attack, but he managed to swing his ax at the beast and kill it before he lost his own life. She could tell he was a trapper by the fur hat which had been knocked off his head and the other clothing he wore made of animal skins. Ahmeya examined the trees above him. He must have been cutting this dead tree, and when it fell, it struck the other tree. The broken top of the tree had then come straight down and pinned him before he could get out of the way. She felt sorry he had died that way even though he was a white man. Before long, he would probably be eaten by another wolf, or perhaps a bear would smell his carcass.

She had not been close to a white man in all the time she had lived with the Lenape and Seneca and, curious, she knelt near him to look at his face. *He must have died recently, there is no smell of death yet.* Instinct told her to hold her hand in front of his nose, and when she did, she felt the very faint exhale of his breath. Realizing he was still breathing, she jumped up suddenly and stepped back from him. "You are alive." She studied the woods around her. There, just over another rise, she spotted the roof and sides of a cabin. Maybe there is someone to help him, she wondered. Then, realizing the state his body was in, he must have laid there for days. If there were another person around, they would have found him by now. He must be alone.

"What should I do?" she asked aloud. All was still in the woods around her. No answer came except the loud warning squawking of a blue jay. *He is so severely injured and so close to his spirit leaving his body, I should just walk away. This is an evil white man like the soldiers who killed my family.* She approached the body again, put her foot on his shoulder, and pushed. There was no response. His spirit is almost ready to leave. *I should let the Great Spirit Kishelemukong have his way with him, or perhaps his spirit will restlessly wander the earth forever as punishment.*

Ahmeya went back to where she had left Kuskusky and started to walk on, feeling somewhat sad that the white man was going to die in a crushing accident like that. "We must leave him Kuskusky; there is nothing we can do," she told her daughter. She continued to walk away, holding Kuskusky's hand over another rise and then another until she was far from the tragic scene. It continued to trouble her, though. *What if Tamataunee had an accident like that with no one to help him? I would want someone to help his spirit pass to the afterworld, even if it were an enemy. No, I am sure he will give up living soon. I do not need to give him a better place to die. It is useless to help him; it would be a waste of my time to stay, and it would delay us from our journey to reach the Cayuga.* She walked on for some time longer, justifying in her mind the reason to leave the white man lying there, then feeling guilty because she would not even walk away from an animal to suffer a slow death that way. She loudly cursed her bad luck, turned around, and headed back.

When she returned to the scene a couple hours later, nothing was different. The man appeared to be dead and was unresponsive to even hard shaking just as when she had left him, but he still had breath. She got Kuskusky settled in a safe place while she figured out what to do. Her first problem was to get the treetop's heavy bulk off his legs. She tried picking one end up, but the weight of it was too much for her to move even a little. The man had hacked away at the log and tried to dig underneath it with no luck. His hands were covered in dirt, and his fingernails were bloodied and broken. Ahmeya studied the problem of getting the weight off him for several minutes. She would need that ax he had clutched in his hand. Carefully, watching his face closely, she pulled the ax handle from his grip. There was no resistance or movement, not even a twitch. She used the ax to cut a strong straight limb from a tree nearby and gathered a pile of rocks. Little by little, using the limb and stones as a lever, she pried the log higher and higher by putting all her weight on the lever to raise it and then jamming more rocks beneath the log so it would stay up. Kuskusky helped by handing her stones. It only rose slightly each time, and it took her some time and lots of effort, but finally, it was clear enough for her to pull the man out from beneath the broken treetop.

She knelt, hooked her arms around his shoulders, and dragged him free. Standing there with her arms at her sides, she stared down at him. *Well, I guess I better check his injuries,* she thought, and as she pulled up his pant legs, she saw both his legs were severely broken as she had guessed. Ahmeya had seen broken bones before while living with the Lenape. Mahonoy had been the herbalist for the tribe and had prescribed lots of remedies for injuries, but Ahmeya had never seen damage this severe. She wondered if his legs were crushed beyond being saved. *He will die anyway, he is injured so severely, and his spirit wants to leave his body. Why am I doing this?* She put her hand close to his nose again. He still had a faint shallow breath. *No, I cannot leave him out here on the ground for the animals. Somehow, I must get him into that cabin.* In there, his body would not be ripped apart by wild animals before he died. Using his felling ax again, she fashioned a traverse out of saplings and vines to put him on so she could drag him over the ground to the building. It was difficult, but she managed to roll his lifeless body onto the traverse. The land was uneven, and many trees and stumps were in the way as she pulled the traverse. It took all her strength, but eventually, she was in an open area in front of his cabin.

She stepped onto the small porch area and opened the door. No one was inside. She went back to the man and, putting her arms under his shoulders again, she dragged his body up onto the platform and then into the cabin. She wrinkled her nose when she leaned in close to him. "Oh, you smell." He was a disgusting and unclean, smelly wretch with his matted sweaty hair and the dirt he had been laying in. He must have been pinned there dying for days. Once inside, Ahmeya left him lying on the floor and turned to check on Kuskusky. She was already inside and happily exploring the cabin, oblivious to the seriousness of what was happening around her. Ahmeya sat down in a chair and studied the man while she tried to catch her breath. It had been a lot of work to get him inside that cabin, but she was not done yet.

"Now, what am I going to do?" She wondered aloud, looking at the lifeless man. "He will die soon, but better in here than out there for a wolf or bear to eat while he still has breath." Looking at the awkward angles his legs were laying, she thought, *I should straighten those legs.* She walked over to where he lay and used her knife to cut up the front of his pantlegs one at a time. Both legs were crushed and badly broken from his knees down. There were dark purple bruises and bumps where bone had been dislodged from where it should be and pushed out against the skin. *At least there is no open wound or blood loss, although I do not know what has happened to his insides.*

The color of his legs below the breaks was pale from lack of circulation, and she wondered if his legs could be saved at all if he did live. She felt it was a waste of effort to try to do anything for him, but the compassion she had in her heart for any injured creature compelled her to do something just as it had drawn her back. She decided to try to straighten his legs and splint them. She went outdoors and took some saplings from the traverse. Using his felling ax, she cut them into shorter lengths that would fit alongside his legs and brought them back inside.

She needed something to tie the saplings onto his legs. She found an empty sack and ripped it into strips of cloth. Kneeling beside him, she grimaced with the thought of how much it would hurt if he woke up and felt the pain of what she was about to do. Would he attack her? It took a lot of pressure and all the weight she could muster to press on his leg bones and force each leg back into what she hoped was a normal position. She pushed and felt along each bone to be sure they were lined up correctly and cussed at the man for making her do that. She kept watching his face, but there was still no sign of movement or reaction of any kind.

Satisfied she had done her best, she strapped two saplings onto each leg to keep them straight and tied them tight with the strips of cloth. She stood up, put her hands on her hips, and scrutinized her work. "There, the rest is up to the Ancestors." She was exhausted from how much physical exertion it had taken to get him into the cabin and set his broken legs. Now, she checked on Kuskusky and saw her handling some metal animal traps. Ahmeya rushed to stop her before she got hurt and told her firmly, "Do not touch them." She scooped Kuskusky up into her arms and sat back down with her. Then she looked around at the single room of the trapper's cabin.

There was a bed against a wall made of wood posts with crisscrossing ropes that held a stuffed mattress. "I should get this man onto that bed," she told Kuskusky, "but not right now." There was a stand under a small window that held a washbasin with a dirty towel lying beside it. Blackened cooking pots and a few tin plates and cups were piled on a shelf along with crocks and a few bags of food stores. Some dingy looking clothing, traps, and miscellaneous gear hung from pegs on one wall. A large fieldstone fireplace with a stone hearth had a crude wood mantle over it. Ahmeya suddenly had a strong feeling of something familiar. An empty cobalt blue glass bottle with sunlight coming through it sat on a small windowsill and was draped with a spiderweb that connected to the sash. There was another chair at the fireplace, and an oval braided rug lay in front of it. On a small rustic table was a dusty book with the word Bible on the cover. Beside the bible lay an embroidery hoop with some cloth, yarn, and a needle stuck in it, all equally dusty. Ahmeya had been in cabins before. Many of the Seneca lived in cabins, but none looked like this inside.

Waves of remembrance swept over Ahmeya as she looked around, and long-lost scenes from her own childhood came creeping back like the mist that gradually covered the earth some evenings. She saw a powder horn hanging on a peg and a long rifle over the door and remembered her father, Cornelius, again with great sadness. The cabin was unkempt and dirty like what a trapper might have, but this was not just a man's cabin. It had the mark of a woman on it also. Clutter, dust, and cobwebs were evidence the woman's touch was missing. Ahmeya wondered where she was. Perhaps she had gone back to wherever she lived to spend time with her family. Settlers sometimes returned home for visits when the loneliness and separation from family became too much for their souls to bear at times on the frontier.

The cabin and its interior were jolting reminders in Ahmeya's mind of her true heritage. She sat there wearing her colorful Lenape fabric clothing hugging her dark-skinned Lenape daughter in this white man's world, and for the first time, felt conflicted about who she was. "This life is what I came from with my own mother, Ina, and my father, Cornelius. I lived in a cabin like this with my brothers Rubin and little Christopher. I remember now, it was somewhat bigger than this one but so similar." She told Kuskusky. Then she wondered, *where is my mother now? Is she still alive?* She recalled Rubin's death when he fell over the cliff and the separation from her mother when another Indian took her away to the River of Pines in a canoe. Then a strong wave of longing to see her own mother came over her. It was difficult for her to picture her face now after so many years had passed. She wanted to speak to her and show her Kuskusky, her granddaughter. She wanted to tell her about Mahonoy, her Indian mother, who had adopted and taken good care of her all these years. Most of all, she wanted to tell her about Tamataunee. He had brought her such joy and love and given her Kuskusky. "It has been so long since I saw my mother. I miss seeing her face and hearing her voice. I miss her hugs and goodnight kisses." she told Kuskusky sadly. "She used to read me stories before a fireplace like this one. You have another grandmother you do not even know." A tear spilled over its boundary and slowly traveled down Ahmeya's cheek.

It had been so many years since Ahmeya had thought of her colonial family. Those memories had all been locked away in a secret corner of her mind like a protected treasure from long ago when she became adopted. She feared if she let it out, something would snatch her treasured memory away, and it would be gone forever as if her family had never existed. On one wall of the room hung a small carved wooden cross. She remembered evenings when her mother read bible stories aloud to her and her brothers and the verses they learned to recite as their education. She had not thought of her birthplace in such a long time. Now, being in this cabin, it was all coming back.

It was getting late and the room darkened. She decided they would stay in this man's cabin for the night. He owed her shelter for helping him that day. Perhaps by morning, he would finally be dead, and she could walk on and leave him without feeling guilty. Right now, they needed some light. She could feel the coolness of the evening, so Ahmeya took small chunks of wood from a pile by the fireplace and built a fire using a flint and steel she found on the mantle. She could not help but wish she had that flint days earlier when she had struggled so much with her little fire bow. When the man died, she would keep the flint. He would not need it. After she had a good flame going, she took a small stick from the fire and lit a candle. More memories came floating back of her mother sewing by candlelight while her father cleaned his rifle. Though she had never been in this man's cabin, it was feeling familiar.

Kuskusky was drowsy. Ahmeya took some of the trapper's furs from a pile and laid them on the floor for her. Kuskusky was soon asleep while holding her little cattail doll. He will not know we used these furs, she thought. Perhaps she would take some of them also when they left the next day. There was some water in a kettle, and Ahmeya heated it by the fire. She found a cup and made some tea from Bee Balm leaves she had saved in her carry bag. She sat in the chair a long time sipping her tea and remembering more of her young life as a colonial girl and then later when she became a Lenape. She looked at the motionless trapper's body, still laying on the floor where she had dragged him in. Now, his splinted legs were laying straight, but there were still no signs of life from him. She felt sure his breathing would stop at any moment. She decided he could stay right where he was. She would not try to move him onto his bed. That would be a wasted effort.

Ahmeya finished her tea and banked the small fire. She blew out the candle and lay down on the floor next to Kuskusky and cuddled her close. She could see the shadowy form of the strange man not far away from her and wondered what tomorrow would bring before she too fell asleep from exhaustion.

Early in the morning, Kuskusky stirred and woke her. For a moment, she did not remember where she was. Then, recalling the day before, she sat up quickly and studied the body of the man. She wondered if he had died and she could leave the cabin and be back on their way. She rose and moved closer to him, she leaned over and put her hand in front of his face to see if there was any breathing. There were still faint exhales coming from his nose. Her shoulders slumped. She cursed his spirit to either stay and walk on the earth or leave and join his Ancestors. She moved his pantlegs and checked his feet and ankles. They were not blue or black, so she knew blood was circulating through his broken and splintered legs. She wondered how long he had laid trapped under that log, then left him to take care of Kuskusky's needs. She was hungry and needed washing up, so Ahmeya gave her some food. There was a container of water and a tin pan along with a bar of lye soap under the small window which Ahmeya used to wash Kuskusky. So, this dirty trapper does have soap to use, she noticed. Then she told Kuskusky to play with her little cattail doll because she had some work to do.

She turned her attention back to the trapper. She should try to give him some water, his lips look so cracked and dry. His mouth was slightly open, and Ahmeya decided to squeeze some water into it from a wet cloth and see if she could trickle some of it between his lips. To her surprise, when she did that, he swallowed. She squeezed out some more water, and again he swallowed, so she spoke to him, but he did not answer. Ahmeya continued to give him a little water at a time until he stopped taking more, and it just ran out the corner of his mouth. She scrutinized his still face. His eyes were closed, so she lifted a lid slightly and asked him loudly in Lenape, "Are you there?" He did not even blink. It was as if his life had left his body, and only a breath remained living in the shell.

Again, she was struck by how dirty and unkempt he was with his dark, tangled, greasy hair and matted overgrown beard. As she studied him, she saw ants crawl out of his hair and skitter across his face. Shuddering, she brushed them away. He was so hairy; he was more like an animal than a man. Carefully she lifted his buckskin shirt to see if he had any other injuries. When she saw the hair on his chest, she was even more sure he was part animal. The Lenape and Seneca men Ahmeya had seen in her tribe did not have facial or chest hair. It was their practice to pluck any sparse hair that did grow; they did not want it. They only left a topnotch of hair on their heads. This white man must be hiding something to grow so much hair to cover his body.

She saw old scars on his torso from long ago injuries and some new red scrapes and fresh bruises, but nothing that appeared to be a troubling injury except his legs, so she covered him back up. With a lot of exertion, she dragged his body over to his bed and managed to lift him onto it. She pulled the quilt from the foot of the bed over him. Standing there looking down at him, she asked Kuskusky, playing happily on the floor, "Now what do we do with him?" Kuskusky just shrugged her shoulders. Ahmeya continued, "We need to keep walking northeast, and yet I cannot leave this wretch of a dying man like this. We should not stop and stay here; we need to be on our journey. Perhaps we will stay another day. Until then, I think we will rest and get stronger to finish our travel to the land of the Cayuga."

CHAPTER 4

AHMEYA WENT BACK OUTSIDE AND PICKED up the ax to split firewood left scattered around a stump. She swung the ax from high above her head and came down on the wood with all the power she could muster. It felt good to see the man's firewood split and torn into pieces, and she continued chopping until she had a generous pile ready to be burned. She loaded up her arms and took it inside. Every so often, she gave the man a little more water squeezed from a wet cloth until he did not swallow anymore. She kept busy picking up grungy clothes and pelts thrown around the cabin. Dangerous traps were scattered here and there, and she put them on pegs out of her daughter's reach. In a corner, she was surprised to see a bow and quiver of arrows. She could tell it had belonged to an Indian by how it had been made and the native American beaded decorations on the deerskin quiver holding the arrows. Ahmeya had observed Tamataunee craft bows and arrows similar to them. It troubled her that the trapper had something that obviously did not belong to him. Had he taken that bow and quiver from an Indian he had killed? After seeing them, she was even more distrustful of the man and went to where he lay to check for weapons. Feeling his side, she found a large knife in a sheath and carefully removed it while watching his face for any signs of movement, but there was none. The knife's handle was made of antler, and the heavy blade had a curve on the end for ripping open an animal's skin and flesh. She hid the knife but would remember where it was in case she needed it to defend herself.

Early in the evening, Ahmeya made a simple soup by boiling corn kernels from a dried ear of corn she found hanging from the ceiling. She added salted, dried meat from his stores, and cooked the two together. It made a good meal for her and Kuskusky, then remembering the man she let some cool, scooped up a little liquid and slowly spooned it into his half-opened mouth. He continued to swallow the warm broth until he had taken a small amount. Again, Ahmeya demanded of him, "Come back to the living, open your eyes or leave this world!" But as before, there was no movement or sign that he had heard her pleas.

The trapper was so pale looking, Ahmeya thought Manetuwak or an evil spirit would take his soul away at any moment, but she had started something now and must try to help him. Doing otherwise might bring bad luck onto her and Kuskusky. She placed peace offerings to the spirits all around him. Tobacco she had found in a round tin was placed on his chest, and she put colorful beads from her small pouch by the tobacco. She laid stones that sparkled with white quartz at his sides along with fragrant wintergreen leaves. She had collected dark berries from a pokeberry plant, crushed them, and used the red juice to make wide diagonal lines and other symbols on his cheeks and forehead to please the spirits. She sang songs to the Creator God Kishelemukong and danced in the manner that she had seen Mahonoy do while healing others. The next day Ahmeya gathered bark from the side of a tree where the morning sun gave it strength and healing. She used her knife and carved symbols of turtle and other spirit animals on the bark and lay it around his legs. A small bundle of sacred herbs was tied together, lit on fire, and she fanned the smoke over his body from head to toe with turkey feathers. It was up to Kishelemukong now. She did not know what the white man had done to cause an evil spirit to hurt him this way any more than what she had done to suffer the loss of her Lenape family and have the loneliness that hurt her so now.

She had no sachem, Meteina, to call upon for help. The trapper should be purified in a sweat lodge, but it was impossible to move him to one now even if she built one. When she finished, the trapper was surrounded by spirit gifts, herbs, and talismans north, south, east, and west all around his body. She stepped back and surveyed her work. She hoped he had a strong spirit guide who would lead him to heal or let him pass to the afterlife to be with his Ancestors if he deserved it. She prayed for something to happen either way so she could leave the man and continue on her way. *Did I do enough?* She wondered as she left his side and sat in the chair. The dusty bible lay on the table beside her, and she opened it randomly.

Ahmeya turned the pages looking for any familiar words. Some folded papers fell from the holy book onto her lap. Picking up the papers, she discovered they were covered with ink drawings of plants and descriptions of them. They were lovely drawings, and Ahmeya recognized the plants when she studied them. One was a drawing of a delicate Columbine bloom suspended from the shepherd's crook of its small stem. Another was a sketch of a Painted Trillium with its three white petals, red center, and broad leaf. Looking through more pages, she saw the heart-shaped leaves of Wild Ginger and a beautiful drawing of a Moccasin Orchid. These drawings must have made by the woman who lives here, she realized, and that person must have loved the forest plants and wild places as much as I do.

The drawings must have meant a lot to the woman to tuck them into the holy book. Ahmeya carefully folded the treasured drawings and placed them back between the pages, and as she did, she noticed a verse had been marked. She read it slowly, sounding out the words, 'Behold, I have given you every plant yielding seed that is on the face of all the earth, and every tree with seed in its fruit. You shall have them for food.' Ahmeya remembered she had learned that same verse many years ago from her mother and could almost recall the sound of her voice as she read.

A couple days passed and Ahmeya kept checking on the trapper and giving him water and broth. At times she went outside with Kuskusky to take walks in the woods around the cabin and continue gathering wild foods and healing and cooking herbs. She planned to dry everything she could collect before a frost destroyed the plants. It was the time to harvest such things, and she would need dried foods for their journey. During the day, she kept a small fire going for cooking and to have warmth at night. The trapper was still unconscious, but because of her, he was lying in his bed under a quilt. She and Kuskusky still slept on furs on the floor where they were comfortable. It felt much like the sapling platforms they slept on in their longhouse. On one of her excursions into the woods, she recognized the dying yellow leaves of ginseng with its bright red berries. Mahonoy had taught her the root of this plant was powerful medicine for healing and strength. They were even the shape of a man's body to further indicate they were meant for healing, and she dug several. It was an important find that she hoped would help him. Whatever she gathered, she showed to Kuskusky, thanked the spirit of the plant, and told her its name and use just as Mahonoy had done for Ahmeya. While they were out gathering, she noticed squirrels scampering and arguing over hickory, walnut, beechnuts, and acorns that were falling to the ground everywhere and she and Kuskusky collected them as well.

Still in need of meat, she made another snare and set it up to catch the squirrels she saw around the nut trees. She marked the tree and bent over the ends of branches on her way to the cabin so she could find it quickly again. When she checked the next day, she had caught a plump grey squirrel. That made her happy because they were larger and meatier than a red squirrel. She reset the snare and then cleaned the squirrel carcass for cooking later. One was not enough for them, so she set another snare. When she checked later, she had more grey squirrels to add to supper that night. The trapper did not have much for food stores, so she felt the need to get more food. If he died, she would take whatever she could find in the cabin and continue her journey. He would not need food any longer.

That evening she got another ear of corn, scraped the hard kernels off the cob, ground them, and put the meal into boiling water. She threaded the gutted and cleaned squirrel carcasses onto a stick and roasted them over the fire. Ahmeya and Kuskusky had a good meal and she felt refreshed and pleased she had provided for her daughter once more. She made a thin broth with squirrel meat and ginseng root and tried feeding it to the Trapper with a spoon. He had not opened his eyes since she had come upon him pinned under the log. Even what must have been the extremely painful resetting of his broken legs had not brought him out of his unconscious state, yet he was swallowing the broth. His face was close to hers as she spooned it carefully into his mouth while propping his head up with her other hand. Ahmeya was suddenly startled to see him open his eyes and look at her. "Ahh, there is still a spirit in your body," she said to him. After just a few swallows, he stopped taking more broth and closed his eyes.

That night Ahmeya picked the bible up again. There was a page inside the front cover with handwritten names and dates. Ahmeya remembered her mother writing on a page like that in her bible. As a little girl living with her mother, Ina, and father, Cornelius, she had not read often. She preferred being outdoors exploring the fields and woods or playing in a stream, but her mother had insisted she spend time each day learning to read by reciting verses from the bible and children's poems. She studied the neat writing on the page and read *'Zebulon Elias Warfle wedded to Bridgette Maria Klinges on May 15th, 1778.' That must be this trapper!* She wondered silently, *where is Bridgette?* She turned more pages. Now, so many years later, after not seeing printed words for so long, it was difficult, but words came back to her. She sounded out a few, but so many others were beyond her comprehension. She closed the bible and put it back.

Kuskusky was already asleep lying on the furs. Her sweet, innocent little child was lying there so peaceful while Ahmeya was so full of turmoil and anger at being forced to stay there. Ahmeya looked over at the trapper. She was startled to see he had turned his head and was staring directly at her. There was confusion and danger in his eyes, then he closed them, and all she saw was the slight rise and fall of his chest. It was unsettling to see him look at her that way, but she knew there was no chance he would get off that bed and harm her or Kuskusky. There was a banging noise against the cabin, and she heard a strong wind howling along with rain pelting the roof. Except for those sounds, the cabin was quiet, and she was thankful they had a warm, dry place to rest and were not out there in the anger of the storm. She nervously glanced over at the sleeping man again. Thankfully he had fallen back into a deep sleep, and she blew out the candle and lay down on the floor beside Kuskusky.

Ahmeya woke to the sound of loud cursing from the trapper. He was struggling to sit halfway up while clutching at his legs.

He glared at Ahmeya menacingly and shouted, "What have you done to me squaw? I cannot move my legs!" He tried to lift one leg, then gave up and fell backward against the bed groaning in pain. Feeling some objects by his head and face, he was puzzled by the different things surrounding his body and legs. "What the hell is this?" He asked as he picked up pieces of bark and stones.

Ahmeya got up and went cautiously nearer to him. "You were hurt, I found you pinned beneath brother tree," she spoke to him in Lenape. "I gave you strong medicine from the spirits of the woods and four directions of the earth." She said, pointing to the herbs, bark, and other items she had placed around him." She tried to make him understand that both his legs were badly broken. Ahmeya was glad he could not see the bright red lines and symbols she had painted on his cheeks and forehead.

The trapper had traded with the Seneca Indians nearby and could speak some of their language. Though he was not fluent in native tongues, he understood enough to know what she was saying. He examined the sapling splints tied on his legs and realized this squaw must have helped him.

He did not have contact with natives often but thought the Seneca were good to trade with. He would give them something they needed, such as fishhooks, awls, or needles and other items they did not have in exchange for furs to add to what he trapped on his own. It was worthwhile for him to do that when it came time for his annual trip to the buyer. He never let down his guard when trading with them. He had heard too much about raids and killings that had taken place not far away and was careful whenever he was around them. He was wondering right now if this squaw was alone or if there was a brave with her ready to kill him? Yet, all he saw with her was a little girl.

Being cautious, he checked for his knife and realized it was not there, the sheath was empty. "Damn thieves!" he uttered aloud, scowling at her. Ahmeya had noticed him searching for his knife and was thankful she had taken it from him earlier.

"Why are you here squaw, who the hell are you?" he asked Ahmeya in an angry voice. She told him she was walking north to join some other Seneca and came across him lying in the woods.

"Are you alone? Is someone with you?" he asked, wondering how he had gotten into his bed. She ignored that question, turned around, and stirred up the coals in the fireplace. She could not say the words out loud that *yes, she was all alone and on her own.* He stopped talking and she got busy heating up broth with rabbit meat for Kuskusky and the man. The trapper was terribly weak but did mumble that he was hungry, which was a good sign. It was not so easy for her to approach him now that his eyes were open, and he was talking. She had felt no danger when he was unconscious, but now this white man was awake, moving some, and speaking to her. She kneeled by the bed and tried to spoon broth into his mouth as before, but he reached up angrily, gave her an ugly look, and ripped the spoon from her hand. His hand trembled, and the broth spilled into the wildness of his unkempt beard and onto his chest. He yelled out, "Damnation!" when it happened and slumped back. Without a word, she took the spoon from his hand and patiently continued to feed him. They did not speak during that time, and she avoided making eye contact with him. She could feel his seething anger. Shortly after swallowing some broth, he fell back to sleep, and she left his side.

Later that day, she fed him more broth and then checked on his legs. She lifted the quilt and checked his feet. There was no sign of infection and his feet felt warm to her touch, so his blood must be moving in them. She decided to get boneset leaves and make a poultice for his legs. Then she and Kuskusky could leave this wretched man soon and be on their way. During the afternoon, she and Kuskusky went into the woods to hunt for the boneset leaves. The plants still had white blooms on them, and she was lucky to spot them in a wet area. She also gathered some willow bark that she would make into a tea to ease his pain.

Mahonoy had explained how to identify the bone healing herb boneset.

"See how the stalk goes right through the diamond-shaped leaves? It is just how a bone goes through muscle," she had told her. "Our Great Father Kishelemukong gave us this plant to heal bones." Mahonoy had taught her about so many plants and herbs. She had also taught her what berries and plants to stay away from because they would make you sick or take your spirit away. She remembered when Mahonoy stopped her from tasting the shiny red berries of Nightshade.

"No, not them!" she said firmly as she took the berries from Ahmeya's hand. "These are from the evil spirit Manetuwak to trick you. There are good and bad spirits in all things, even something like fire. It can be our friend and keep us warm like a fur blanket, it can be our helper to cook our food, or it can be a beast and eat us with its red, hungry mouth. You must look for the good that is given to us by Kishelemukong and never let an evil spirit trick you again."

Ahmeya thought about the white man lying on his bed. Did he come from Manetuwak to trick me?

Before night fell, she made a boneset poultice by mashing leaves and then applying it to both his legs, although he complained and did not understand how a bunch of green leaves could help him. Ahmeya had seen Mahonoy do this to others that had broken bones, and it had healed them. It was a good, strong medicine. The next day the trapper managed to sit more upright, and it was easier for him to swallow food. Ahmeya knew he was getting better, and it would not be long before he would try walking. She made him a pair of crutches from ash saplings and put them by his bed.

They hardly spoke. Ahmeya just did what she needed to give him nourishment, then left his side and took care of Kuskusky. He made no effort to ask anything about her or give her any information about himself, and she did not want to know. Ahmeya knew she was not welcome and felt she had lost too much time already helping this strange, angry white man who looked and smelled like an animal. She had proven to herself she did not need a man unless it was Tamataunee and could take good care of Kuskusky on her own.

One evening as she was getting Kuskusky ready for bed and braiding her hair, she noticed how tangled it was. She wished she had bear grease for them. It always made their hair so shiny and easier to take care of. Someone in their tribe always had bear grease to share for cooking or other uses. The meat Tamataunee provided them tasted so good when cooked in bear grease seasoned with maple sugar. Ahmeya got a hairbrush she had seen on a shelf in the cabin and started brushing Kuskusky's hair. Suddenly she heard a shout from the trapper.

"No, do not touch that!" he yelled. Both Ahmeya and Kuskusky jumped and were surprised by the hostility in his words. Immediately Ahmeya returned the brush to its resting place as he glared at her. Ahmeya did not know why he was so upset and angry but was sure it involved the woman who owned the hairbrush. The trapper yelled at her again.

"What the hell did you do with my knife squaw? I know you took it, and I want it back."

She hesitated, should she give it back to him?

He added, "I will not hurt you with it; I just want my possessions left where they are supposed to be, Goddammit!"

Feeling that he was being honest, Ahmeya went over to where she had hidden the knife behind a large crock, got it out, and reluctantly handed it back to him. He took it from her hand with a satisfied look and did not say anything. His outburst had helped Ahmeya decide what she was going to do the next day.

After she and Kuskusky woke the next morning, she gave the man some food then went out. She drew water from the well in a bucket, took it inside, and set it by his bedside along with a cup he could use. He still alternated between being awake and resting, but she was sure he was going to live now and was stronger. During one of his wakeful moments, she asked him if she could have a few furs for Kuskusky.

He hesitated, glanced at Kuskusky, and then told her, "Yes, a few, but only some coyote and raccoon and not any beaver." He felt he owed the squaw something, but not his most valuable pelts. When he fell asleep again, Ahmeya got the furs and gathered up her belongings. She took Kuskusky by the hand and went out the door. Before she closed it behind her, she took one last look around the cabin and the sleeping trapper. He will be alright without me now. He will probably get up from bed and start helping himself if I leave. She closed the door behind her and walked away. Looking at the sun's location for direction, she walked into the forest and headed northeast once again.

Ahmeya walked for over four hours before she stopped to rest. She was keeping the trapper with the broken legs out of her thoughts and just focused on her goal of walking northeast. Every time his predicament came into her head, she shut it out by thinking how safe she and Kuskusky would be when they reached the Cayuga. They were sitting on a fallen log to let them both rest their legs when the image of the trapper lying in his bed came into her mind again. Not far away, she saw the skeletal bones of an animal. They had been stripped of all meat, scattered, and left to bleach white in the sun. She thought about the man she had left to fend for himself and suddenly felt remorse for not staying a few days longer until she was sure he was strong and able to move around. Her mind was telling her that she had to leave him to reach the Cayuga before cold weather sets in, but her heart was still feeling compassion for someone that had been so severely injured. She watched Kuskusky playing for a while, then turned her face upwards towards the heavens.

"My Lenape Mother, what shall I do?" she asked her ancestor. "Give me a sign," she pleaded. The trapper might still die if he is too helpless to get nourishment for himself. Maybe his legs will not heal, and he will never be able to walk again, she thought. I would be responsible for killing him even though he is a wretched white man. It would not be good for me to harm his spirit if he had not harmed mine. An evil spirit might take revenge on Kuskusky or me. She sat silent wanting so much to be able to see Mahonoy or Tamataunee's face and have them advise her on what to do. Then she observed the white skeleton bones again and realized that was her sign. He would die unless he had help to defend himself from evil spirits that would take his life. Reluctantly, feeling the burden of it all and knowing the delay would seriously jeopardize her goal of reaching the Cayuga soon, she took Kuskusky by the hand, turned around, and headed back to the trapper's cabin.

It was almost dark when Ahmeya finally returned. She had left the trapper alone for the whole day. When she pushed open the door, she was shocked to see he had tried to get up off his bed but had fallen into a heap on the floor. He had tipped over the bucket of water, and it had poured out across the floor where he was laying in it passed out. For some reason, he had tried to drag his body through the water to cross the room but did not make it. Why would he do such a stupid thing? She wondered. She went over to see if he had hurt himself in addition to the injuries he already had. She shook him slightly to waken him, and he eyed her with that confused stare again. Then he recognized her face and seemed to be relieved. He was still frail, although trying to appear strong, and Ahmeya knew that he could not help himself; she should not have left him.

Ahmeya was just an average size woman, but she was strong, and once again, she had to use that strength to lift him back onto his bed. He winced and grimaced in pain as she moved him. After she had him settled back in bed and covered up and resting, she sat next to the fireplace and let out a long, deep sigh. *This is the fate the Great Spirit has given me. I must care for this trapper until I can leave. I must accept this as my test from the Ancestors until it is finished.* She had walked far that day with Kuskusky before turning around and returning to the cabin. They were both exhausted, and soon she and Kuskusky were resting on furs on the floor as if they had never left.

Days of slow progress in his recovery went by while Ahmeya cared for the man. She helped him stand one day by first having him lean his weight on her and then use the crutches. Bit by bit, his strength returned, and he was doing more to take care of himself. They spoke a few words to each other, no more than what was needed to answer a question or make a request. Whenever she was near him, she was still reminded of how much he was like the animals he trapped: hairy, smelly, unclean, and surly. The Lenape believed in washing daily to keep evil spirits away, so he was especially offensive to her in his state. She could tell he depended on her help, but he never voiced his appreciation for it.

After some time, Ahmeya took the sapling splints off his legs and replaced them with smaller, curved pieces of bark so he could bend his knees. She turned her back and told him to take his trousers off so she could sew them back up where they had been cut open. He covered himself with a quilt while she sat by the fire and sewed the repairs to the deerskin trousers he wore. Kuskusky went over to the foot of his bed, lifted the covers off his feet, and felt them. She touched his toes with her small fingers and ran them across the bottom of his feet. She had seen Ahmeya do that many times to see if the trapper's feet were warm and if the blood was circulating and was only mimicking her mother. The trapper smiled and squirmed as Kuskusky's little fingers tickled his feet. That was the first time Ahmeya had seen the man smile. Ahmeya called Kuskusky away from the trapper. She did not want her daughter to be near the angry man.

"It is okay," he said.

But Ahmeya still worried about how the trapper had gotten that Seneca bow and arrows hidden in the corner and wondered if he was not a dangerous enemy of her people.

Later that night, Ahmeya opened the bible again and tried to read out loud to Kuskusky as her mother Ina had done to her when she was a young girl. Without realizing it, she had opened the book to the Lord's prayer. She started reading, *The Lord is my shepherd . . . I shall not want . . ."* and the words she had memorized with her mother's coaching so many years before came flowing back to her. She read on, reciting at times only from memory, and when she got to the *part "Yay, though I walk through the valley of death, I shall fear no evil . . ."* She heard the trapper's voice join her own for that verse as he listened across the room. Was he trying to tell her not to be afraid of him? He must have sensed her fear of having her daughter near him. Or could he be hinting that he had been in the valley of death and was not fearful of her because she had saved him?

It was silent, then he quietly asked her, "What is your name, squaw?"

"They call me Ahmeya, " she answered. "But my English name is Amelia. What name do they call you?" she asked him.

"My name is Zeb; This is my cabin. This is my homestead." He was staking out his ownership of the place. Amelia thought he had a strange short name but did not say so. Then he asked, "What were you doing in my woods? Are there more of you hiding around here?"

"I was walking north with my daughter. We are going to the land of the Cayuga, the place of the Great Council Meetings." Amelia told him. There was silence while the trapper absorbed what she was telling him.

"Do you know that is a long distance away, and you must walk over very difficult terrain to travel with many valleys, marshes, and hills?" he asked.

"Yes, I know it is far, but we need to go there. My family is gone, and I want my daughter to be with people like her," she answered. Amelia had lived among the Lenape and Seneca so long she truly felt as if she was also one of them. Besides, after seeing the white soldiers destroy everything she had loved, she no longer considered white people to be her heritage.

"There are also French patrols up in that area and other trappers and hunters, even deserters from the war hiding out. You would get harmed and captured or worse if they saw you walking alone, squaw," he told her.

She knew it was dangerous, but that news was alarming to her. She had not known the French were up north where she was heading and never considered the other dangerous men. She had just wanted to get far away from the soldiers. Now she had an even heavier burden of worry.

"Where did you come from?" Zeb asked her.

Amelia told him about her village at the southern end of Seneca Lake and how she had seen it destroyed by the white soldiers. She also mentioned that they were continuing to march north and were destroying all the Seneca villages, crops, and orchards that they came across. The trapper was shocked at that news and disappointed. He had traded with natives in villages further up for furs he could sell to his buyer in Elmira.

All he expressed to Amelia was, "that is too bad." Then both fell silent.

Amelia wanted to ask him how he had gotten the Seneca bow and arrows but was afraid of what he might answer. She also wanted to ask him why the white men had to destroy everything dear to her and take sacred belongings for themselves, but she did not.

After that evening, they still did not talk much but seemed to come to an understanding that he needed her help, and she could stay until he finally healed enough to take care of himself. Zeb hobbled around with the crutches for a time and then one day set them aside. Days and days passed, though, until he could walk without painful difficulty and move around to get the things he needed on his own. Amelia had chanted many prayers to the ancestors for help in healing him quickly and used all the herbal remedies she could force on him to make him strong. However, by the time he finally walked well enough to go outdoors and do chores such as chopping and bringing in wood, it was mid-October, cold and dismal, and soon the first snows of winter would be falling. Kuskusky was too young to travel when the deep snow and bitter winds of winter came. Amelia had kept busy chopping wood, setting snares for food, cooking, and caring for Kuskusky and Zeb. She realized as the days got shorter and colder that she would be forced to winter at the trapper's cabin until Springtime when the winter weather broke enough for her to walk northeast again.

Zeb was often melancholy, depressed, and moody. Quite often, he was abrupt and unfriendly when talking to her. He had more than his broken legs to get beyond, Amelia realized. He would slam things around in the cabin, and cleanliness or eating regular meals meant nothing to him. One day when she was returning from picking wild crab apples, she saw him sitting on a stump in front of the cabin doing nothing. He leaned over his knees with his head hanging down and shoulders slumped. He was not listening or talking to her. He had gone out to bring wood in for the fire when she left, but the chunks lay in a heap by his feet. Zeb loathed depending on the squaw for help. Since he had lost Bridgette, he had gotten used to living alone. His homestead was his private domain. Now he had been invaded by this Indian squaw and her child. They were wandering around inside the cabin and poking into his things. This squaw Ahmeya, or Amelia, he was not sure what the hell to call her, had moved most of his things to different places. He had known right where he had always left certain traps and gear, and now had trouble finding the most trivial things. Even though his cabin was small, he had to look for things now. He used to just drop his traps and tools wherever he wanted. She picked items like that up and put them out of reach of Kuskusky. Having her stay the winter also meant more food would be needed even though he did appreciate her doing the cooking each day, and she did bring in game. She cooked some strange things gathered from the woods at times, though. Often, he did not know what he was being offered to eat.

What if she poisoned me and took over living in my cabin? She has nothing now; she could really gain by doing that. No, I do not think she would have gone to all the trouble of saving my life only to kill me, he told himself. *But she could change her mind and kill me if it were to her advantage.* He had been told about the cruelties native people had inflicted on settlers when he had been selling furs to the buyer. There were stories of other trappers and traders that the natives had killed and taken all their goods so they could trade or sell them instead. For that reason, he was always cautious when he was trapping or dealing with them and did not let his guard down. If he got into an argument with natives around him, he could be killed by them. However, the natives he had dealt with so far had been friendly and honest people. They had even welcomed him into their home and given him food. He knew many men had joined the fight against the natives, but he had never had problems with the Seneca near him and respected their rights to their land. Zeb had chosen to live a peaceful life and not be part of the battles between the natives and the settlers.

He had enough of war when he fought for the Rhode Island militia before he came to Seneca Lake. In Rhode Island, neighbors wanting the new, independent colonies had fought against their own neighbors and relatives who wished to stay loyal to the King. People they had known for years became their enemies when sides were taken. Zeb had lost all faith in his fellow man when he saw how changed and divided they became and the ease with which they turned on each other so cruelly. A friend he had grown up with sided with the British and fought alongside them against the Rhode Island militia. Friends had killed friends because they disagreed, and it sickened him. As soon as his volunteer time was up, he packed up his belongings, left Little Compton, and headed for the promising lands of the new Military Tract in New York State.

Amelia was half concerned, half annoyed at him when she saw Zeb just sitting on that stump for so long. He had been seated like that when she left over two hours ago. He should be more active now. His legs had healed well, and he hardly limped or complained of pain. He should be moving around and using them more. She stepped up on the small porch to go inside the cabin. She was going to crush the wild apples she had been collecting, take out the cores and seeds, and make little cakes to dry. A sense of mischievousness came over her, and she took a small apple, jammed it onto the end of a flexible stick, pulled it back, and aimed it at the back of his head. He jumped when it bounced off him, turned around while rubbing his head, and glared at her.

Then he reached down, picked up the apple, and yelled, "You better duck!" as he threw it back towards her. He meant to miss, he was not even close to hitting her, but she ducked anyway.

She loaded another small apple onto the stick and sent it flying back at him, yelling, "No, you better duck." He did duck that one, because she was not trying to miss. It was tense for a moment. Ahmeya was not sure what he was going to do. She wondered if she should have flung those apples at him.

Kuskusky was at her side, and the little girl reached into Amelia's basket and threw an apple at him too, and then another and yelled, "You duck."

He pretended he had gotten hit by them and yelled out, "Ouch that hurt." Then he got a big grin on his face, slapped his knees, and started laughing. She and Kuskusky joined in, and soon all three could not stop laughing. "You win," Zeb told them as they gave up and went into the cabin. Then he picked up the firewood and carried it inside.

CHAPTER 5

AFTER THAT DAY, AMELIA AND ZEB put up with each other while doing their daily chores. She did not ask to stay, and he did not tell her to go. She felt safe enough about him having a knife. That did not alarm her anymore, and neither did him having a rifle. She remained troubled, however, about how he had gotten that bow and quiver. Zeb started going away from the cabin trapping again, and they did not spend much time together during the day. Amelia had noticed a great sadness in Zeb's eyes, and sometimes he stared off into the distance as if in deep thought or in another time.

She recognized his melancholy as something like her own pain at losing Tamataunee and Mahonoy, although she did not know what deeply troubled him. She dared not ask what his thoughts were. She helped him when he needed her to, but he seldom reached out to connect with her. It was as if she was something functional to be used when required and otherwise left alone. Kuskusky was outgoing, cheerful, and chatty and kept showing Zeb little things she had found, or objects Amelia had given her, such as the spiral shell of a wood snail. Kuskusky would leave him presents on his bed that he would find when he came in from trapping before he went to sleep. Sometimes it was a rock with a fossil of a shell in it, a colored leaf, or a feather from a Quail or other bird. One time it was a little pile of different kinds of pinecones.

On one night, all was quiet and dark in the cabin. The fire was making sparking noises now and then as it flared up, then settled back down. Kuskusky had fallen asleep some time ago, and Amelia was resting as well. He lay there, staring at the ceiling through the darkness when he heard the familiar croak of a bullfrog. It sounded as if it was right next to him. Feeling a movement under the covers down by his knees, he realized Kuskusky had given him another present. He turned his quilt down, and sure enough, the eyes of a big green frog blinked back at him. He could not help but smile at the little girl's generosity to him even though he did not want to sleep with a frog. He picked it up and set it onto the floor so she could have it back in the morning. It hopped away into the dark. He would thank her for what was genuine thoughtfulness from the sweet girl and not a mean trick.

Kuskusky had a curious mind and often asked Zeb one question after another. She loved spending time outdoors and was especially interested in nature and the animals in the woods around her. Some of her questions were: Does a bear snore like him when it sleeps in winter? How come a frog never jumps backward? Where does the brown go when an ermine turns white? And how can a fish see to swim in the dark? He did his best to answer, but many times he did not know the answers. That got him wondering and curious about those questions himself.

Amelia had stocked up a good supply of foodstuffs by late fall. She had even found a beehive using the method Mahonoy had taught her. She chopped off a stick about three feet long and made a point on one end. She chose a place that still had some late asters and goldenrod blooming, pushed the point into the ground, and dabbed some syrup made from sugar and water on top of the stick. Then she waited for a honeybee to come. Before long, some bees came for the sweetness. Using the tip of a feather, she gently dusted the back of one bee with white powder and watched what direction it flew away. Then she patiently waited for it to return, and when the bee with the white powder came back after only a short time, she knew there was a hive somewhere nearby.

After the same bee left for a second time, she moved the stick further away towards the direction it had flown. The marked bee returned sooner the next time, so she knew she was moving in the right direction, closer to the hive. It took some time and a lot of patience, but she kept watching for the same bee to return to the syrup and moved the stick when it left each time until she finally heard bees buzzing somewhere near her. Following that sound, she found the beehive inside an old dead beech tree. She would need more help now to get the honey. Also, Kuskusky was with her, and she dare not endanger her by angering the bees. She studied the area so she would remember where the hive was, made a mark on a tree nearby, and bent over the tips of some branches as she went back. When she saw Zeb, she told him about the beehive and asked for his help. Would he hold a smoking torch so she could get some honeycombs for them?

"I have not had honey in a long, long time, are you sure it is safe to do that?" When she assured him she had done it before, he told her, "Alright, I will help you, just tell me what to do." Amelia instructed him to make a smoking torch that would calm the bees by packing pine pitch, moss, and herbs on the end of a stick. She made a couple bark containers to put some honeycombs in and asked Kuskusky to help carry them because they were going to get a treat. They headed back to the bee tree following the markings she had left to find the way. Amelia found a safe place away from the bee tree where Kuskusky was in no danger of being stung. She told her to stay right there, not to come any closer. She and Zeb got ready to get some honey. Zeb lit the torch, and soon it was filling the surrounding air with smudgy billows of smoke.

When Amelia approached the tree, she started talking to the bees, telling them what she was going to do, and thanking them for sharing their food. "I will not take all your sweet goodness, Brother Bees," she told them. Zeb stood way back and stretched out his arm with the smoldering torch to calm the bees as Amelia reached into the hive. Bees crawled onto her hands and arms, but she was not getting stung as she talked calmly to them and moved slowly. Zeb just watched, amazed at what she was doing.

She filled the two baskets she had brought with honeycombs that dripped with amber sweetness and then slowly stepped back to join Zeb. "Keep the torch going. They will be restless for some time, Zeb," she told him. Slowly and quietly, they walked away with neither getting stung. She called Kuskusky to join them and let her taste the sticky honey on her fingers. Then Amelia held out a honey-covered finger to Zeb for him to taste. He hesitated, and then he held her hand, put her finger in his mouth, and sucked the honey off her finger.

He smacked and licked his lips. "Oh, that is good."

Teasing him, she replied, "I told you I could do it." Amelia smugly smiled and held her head high as she turned around and walked away. Zeb trailed along behind her shaking his head in disbelief at what he had just seen.

At times, Amelia saw a spark of humanity in Zeb, and her feelings about him started to soften. He would listen attentively to Kuskusky talk to him and smile at her. He would even reach out and stroke her little head and pat her back. The darkness of his depression was lifting. Mornings started frosty now with ice crystals or newly fallen snow clinging to the branches of the pine and hardwood trees like frosting. Ice crystals sparkled and flashed when the sun hit them. The tree limbs were bare except for the pines and hemlocks. All the hardwood trees had lost their leaves. Only a few clusters of brown beech or oak leaves still clung tight to those trees. She recognized some sugar maples from their shapes and bark and remembered how her Lenape family had gathered the sap to boil into syrup each spring.

What an adventure for the tribe and joyous time of fellowship among them doing that hard work. Amelia decided she would make some maple sugar from those trees next spring before she left, and maybe some maple snow candy for Kuskusky. In the back of her mind, she prayed the trapper would not send them out into the cold of winter when the snows got deep. The Great Spirit Kishelemukong was powerful and had helped her get this far, but she knew others died during winter with no proper shelter or food. As much as she disliked any white man, she would do what she must to keep Kuskusky sheltered, fed, and safe.

Often, when Zeb was out trapping, his mind would go back to an earlier time. He had brought his wife Bridgette to this promising area, and they had built this cabin on their homestead together. He had picked out this general area for them to live because there was plenty of game, plenty of pines to fell for building a cabin, and water nearby. He had seen a variety and abundance of game to trap. Bridgette had even been good at dowsing for water, and he cut a forked stick off a wild cherry tree for her to use. When she walked around with the Y shaped stick held just right, it pointed straight down, locating a water vein for a well.

They decided to build the cabin right by it. It had taken him several days to dig the well and lay up its rock walls. Although it was not deep, it turned out to be a dependable source of water just as she told him it would be. They had been so happy working together on their homestead. She removed the bark from the logs he cut and helped him in any way she could. They had worked side by side to raise the walls and get the roof on using ropes and pulleys to maneuver the heavy logs. It was a small cabin to be sure, but they planned to add on to it eventually.

When Bridgette became pregnant to their surprise, they were even happier knowing they were going to be a family. But it was a difficult pregnancy, and she was often ill and bedridden. No one lived close for advice on how to make her feel better. Some days she was too dizzy to even stand up or walk around inside the cabin. He worried a great deal about her falling and hurting herself.

Zeb did what he could to make things easier for Bridgette, but he had no knowledge of what was normal for a woman to be going through during that time. She was a couple of months into her pregnancy when he heard her slurring her words. Then she clutched her head with both hands and cried out in terrible pain. Moments later, she collapsed and was gone. He went to her side immediately but soon realized she had died and there was nothing he could do. He knelt on the floor where she had passed, holding her in his arms until darkness filled the room before he finally carried her lifeless body to their bed. He sat beside her all night, unable to sleep. At times he placed his open palm on her belly and sobbed for them all. The next day he buried her close to the cabin. Zeb had heard of older people dying suddenly like that of a ruptured blood vessel but not one as young as Bridgette. He was bereft at the loss of both his wife and the unborn baby. It was all still so fresh in his mind. After he buried her, he just moped around the cabin for months. He lost weight, not even wanting to eat. He slept long hours and had no desire to do anything. All purpose in living was lost to him. Eventually, he started to come back and vented some of his anger at God by felling trees, a lot of trees, and chopping and splitting the wood.

The day Amelia found him; he had been chopping down another tree. He had plenty of wood stacked by then but needed the hard, physical exertion of felling trees to work out his sadness and anger, so he kept chopping them down. He just wanted to do hard, demanding physical work where too much thinking was not necessary. He had not noticed that the tree he was cutting was heavy limbed on one side. He swung away with his ax, removing a large triangle wedge at the trunk's base, then went around the other side and started making freeing cuts so it would fall where he wanted it. The tree began to go down the way he had planned, but the heavily weighted side suddenly made it twist on its base. When it hit a large dead tree, it broke it in half, and the top came straight down before he could get out of the way. He was pinned beneath it in excruciating pain for days as he tried to move the heavy log off him. He became delirious then unconscious and did not remember anything until he woke up in his bed with splints on both legs and the Indian woman and her child there. He was not sure if he was grateful she had saved his life.

So far, only light snows had fallen interspersed with sunny, warm melting days. Amelia was still able to go out with Kuskusky bundled up in furs to gather some wild provisions, but it was getting difficult now.

Nature was shutting down its cupboard, and soon the earth would be too hard for digging roots and tubers, and everything green would be destroyed. The squirrels and other animals would have taken most of the nuts and acorns. What was left would be buried in snow that would not melt, but just pile up higher and higher with each storm. She was still able to get some quail and squirrel in her snares, even a rabbit, and Zeb was amazed at what she would bring back from her scavenging trips into the woods.

She had dried the white bulbs of leeks, cattail tubers, and so much more that he had not even known was edible. She had smoked strips of meat from the animals caught in her snares to save for later winter use. Plus, she had bundles of bark, roots, and all kinds of herbs hanging to dry from the cabin's rafters for medicinal or cooking purposes. She even caught fish for them before the water at the beaver pond was covered with ice. She used the bark from a slippery elm tree to make storage baskets for her bounty and had several sitting around full of goods. She dug arrowhead roots in wet areas and was thrilled when she came across wild rice growing along the bank and thanked the Great Spirit for providing so generously for them. Ahmeya had covered several areas all around the cabin before she would return each time from foraging, but she never came across a worn path leading northeast to the Cayuga as she had hoped. Now, even if she found that path, it was too late to travel it.

Bridgette had been resourceful too before she had died unexpectedly. She sewed clothes for both of them. There were gingham cloth dresses for her and deerskin and other pelts she made into clothes for him. The cabin smelled so good when she was baking bread, and he always snatched a warm piece from the end of a loaf if he could. Bridgette had worked hard since she was a young girl and knew how to take care of a household. She had been orphaned in Germany, and when she was eleven years old, she came to the United States as a servant with a couple to care for their small child. She had been just a child herself.

By the time she was sixteen, she wanted to have a family of her own. Staying on as her employer's servant meant she would have to stay single, and there would be more work. Two more children were added to her employer's family as the years went by. Her employers were very demanding and forced her to do all the housework plus care for the children's needs. She met Zeb while shopping at the mercantile. After a few more chance meetings, they started to plan how they could spend time with each other and met whenever they could. She fell in love right away and married him after a few weeks, much to the disappointment of her employers. It was not just because Zeb was a way out of her situation; it was because she genuinely loved him and wanted to share the life he talked about and be with him.

Zeb missed her and what they had started together. When he went to the buyer to sell his furs, they would bring back sacks of flour along with some cones of sugar, a small block of salt, and some pretty cloth. He hunted for the rest of their food needs. The fat of the animals was their grease, they ate the meat, and he used furs he trapped to trade for any other things they needed. They even ate the meat from the beaver, raccoon, and other animals he caught. When a 50- or 60-pound beaver was cooked right, the meat was tasty and tender.

The pelts from those big beavers got him the best money or trades for goods too. Beaver was in high demand for making top hats and warm coats in the new cities and especially in England, and his buyer would take all he could bring them. He added deer, fox, coyote, wolf, rabbit, raccoon, muskrat, and bobcat to what he could trap or shoot for furs too. He had only shot one bear since homesteading. That one had been coming in close to the cabin and became dangerous. Probably, the scent of the animal skins he had on stretchers had attracted it. That bear was looking for food and would have ripped his work to shreds in one night. He had to shoot it. He and Bridgette had plenty of meat for winter that year and a warm black bearskin too. It was so unfair for Bridgette to have died at such a young age. Life was cruelly taken from many on the frontier.

Time passed, but Zeb and Amelia had no accurate way of telling what day it was. All a person could do was pay attention to the weather, animals' activities, the length of each day, and the sun's position as it rose and set, to know what time of year it was. Winter was long and arduous as usual. Zeb went out and trapped when he could, and during the evenings, he stretched the pelts, scraped fat and meat off them and salted them before drying. Amelia kept the cabin in order, did the cooking, and took care of Kuskusky. Before bedtime by the light of the fireplace, she told Kuskusky some Lenape stories she had been taught. Kuskusky listened intently as Amelia told her about the Seven Wise Men.

Seven Wise Men were living together in a longhouse of the Lenape. Their people thought they were so wise they came to them day and night with questions.

The Wise Men told each other, "We have to get some peace; they are bothering us day after day. We must go away from this place and travel up on the mountain and turn ourselves into big boulders." The Seven Wise Men did that and were happy living on the mountainside for some time. Then a young hunter needed to rest one day and saw the seven large boulders. He noticed they were different from the other boulders scattered around. He spent some time resting by the large boulders and returned to visit them day after day.

One day he talked to them and they talked back. He was surprised, but the boulders were telling him things he wanted to know. He returned to his village and told others about the wonderful boulders that answered his questions. Others went up the mountain to talk to the large boulders too.

Soon, the Seven Wise Men said, "It is not peaceful here any longer; we must move and change again."

They moved up to the top of the mountain and changed themselves into seven strong cedar trees. The winds blew through their needles, the gentle rains refreshed them, and the sun warmed them.

They were happy and at peace, but others heard the cedar trees singing beautiful songs and were drawn to them. Realizing they were the Seven Wise Men, they started asking them questions again.

"Now, what do we do?" One of the trees asked the others. "We need to be where it is quiet so we can find some peace and not be troubled."

A tree looked up at the sky and said, "We can become stars. Then we can see all the people, but the people cannot come to where we are and bother us."

So that is what they did. Now, you can look up into the sky at night and see the Seven Wise Men looking back down.*

Zeb listened to the stories Amelia told Kuskusky and found himself warming up more to the Lenape mother and her child. He could tell she was a good woman who loved her daughter and took care of her. The snow had been falling for a few months, so he knew it must be close to Christmas time. He had no way to know when Christmas was for sure. Bridgette had kept track of the days for them both. Now, because he had been unconscious when his legs were broken and lost track of time, he had no idea what day it was. As an adopted Lenape, Ahmeya believed one day was the same as another, and there were no special days. There was no sabbath day, no names for days, or end of the week, just seasons to go by. Zeb decided it could be around Christmas time and wanted to do something for Kuskusky. He would make her a bed out of saplings as a gift. He managed to work on it outside, so neither could see what he was doing.

One day he carried it inside and put it against the wall. "There," he said to Kuskusky, "now you can sleep in your own little bed." She was so happy she clapped her hands and ran to Zeb and hugged him around his legs. He also presented her with the Seneca bow and arrows he had kept in the corner. He had cut the bow down to a smaller size for Kuskusky to use. Amelia was pleased and surprised he had been so thoughtful and caring to give presents to Kuskusky, but she still worried about how he had gotten that bow and finally asked him. Zeb told her he had often traded goods for furs with a Seneca named Thanaowyte, whom he admired. The Seneca was always friendly, welcomed him into his home, and offered him food and drink when he visited.

Zeb had noticed the Seneca man had an elderly mother living with him whom he loved dearly. When Zeb told Bridgette about the frail

---

* Paraphrased from a Lenape story by Chief Bob Red Hawk. The seven stars are the Pleiades.

old woman, she made her a shawl of fur and cloth that she embroidered with flowers. Bridgette had never met the old Seneca woman but took the time to make her a gift. Zeb gave it to her on his next trip to the village, and Thanaowyte was so moved he insisted Zeb have the bow and quiver of arrows in return. Zeb had admired the set on a previous trip. He tried to give them back because he knew Thanaowyte needed them, but he insisted Zeb keep them.

"You are good friend, Zeb, not like others. I want you to have these." The Seneca Thanaowyte told him he valued their friendship, and he could make more bows and arrows.

When Zeb told Ahmeya he had traded with the Seneca for the bow and arrows, and it had become a present for his wife, she was especially moved that he would give something that special to Kuskusky. He also surprised Amelia by giving her two beautiful red fox pelts so she could make a warm hat and muffs for her and Kuskusky.

Amelia's opinion of Zeb changed when she learned the source of the Seneca bow and quiver. She had misjudged him. She liked the idea of Kuskusky sleeping on the bed that reminded her so much of the platforms made of saplings her Lenape family had in their longhouse, and told Zeb thank you. She spread furs on the new bed for Kuskusky to sleep on that night. Kuskusky wanted Amelia to lay down in the little bed with her, and both Zeb and Amelia smiled at that impossible idea. Instead, Amelia lay on the floor beside Kuskusky as usual, and they both dozed off into a peaceful sleep.

The next day Amelia felt that she should reciprocate by giving Zeb a gift in return. He had been kind and generous to her child. She had noticed the leather sheath for his knife was cracked and coming apart. When Zeb was out of the cabin, she worked on making him a new one and used some of her favorite blue beads from her headband to decorate it. She added some fringe to the bottom of it and decorative stitching with sinew. The next evening, she presented it to him and thanked him for the little bed he had made for Kuskusky and the furs he had given them. He was surprised and awkwardly just nodded his head when she gave him the sheath and thanked him.

Time passed, and the strain and tension between them were replaced with small signs of friendship. They shared laughter at Kuskusky's playfulness and did helpful things for each other. She could tell that the set of his jaw was not so rigid, and his face was more relaxed. He was letting go of his bitter anger. Zeb had cleaned himself up, although Amelia did not think he did that often enough, and he even used Bridgette's sewing scissors to trim his beard and hair. He was getting over his grief and becoming more interested in what was happening around him instead of just trying to bury his feelings with hard, grueling work.

He and Amelia talked more freely now about everyday things. Amelia understood and believed that Mahonoy and Tamataunee were happy and safe with the Ancestors now and was comforted that she would join them one day. Zeb started showing Amelia what he did as a trapper, and when the weather was nice enough, they would put snowshoes on and walk his traplines. Kuskusky would come along too and walk with small snowshoes Amelia had made for her. Amelia had woven a new backpack for Zeb, which he used to carry his traps and any animals he caught. He showed her how to set the metal traps, put some lure on them to attract an animal, and then hide them with brush and other cover. She thought the trap's mechanisms were fascinating but much more dangerous than the way the Lenape and Seneca built their traps. Her Lenape family had only used traps and snares they made from wood and twine. These metal traps were so efficient and caught many valuable fur animals for Zeb if he set them correctly.

When they were done checking the traps and resetting the sprung ones, they headed back to the cabin. The snow was not deep, so walking had been easy, and you could feel the warmth of the sun even though it was winter.

On the way back, Zeb spotted some grapevines hanging on large beech trees and asked Amelia, "Do you know what they are good for?"

She shook her head no, and he suddenly threw his pack and snowshoes off, ran over to a sturdy vine hanging down, and with a whoop, he jumped up and started swinging on it like an ape. He yelled out to them, "Come on, it is fun, swing along with me."

Amelia could not believe what she was seeing, but it did look like fun. She had not swung on a grapevine since she was a child. She found a vine, just the right size for Kuskusky. She showed her how to hold on to it and pushed her back and forth until Kuskusky learned how to run and then lift her feet so she could make it swing by herself. Then Amelia grabbed a grapevine nearby and started swinging, laughing, and yelling along with the other two.

They were all having a great time until Zeb decided to try another vine that was not firmly attached to the tree above it. He pushed himself off from the tree trunk and was swinging back and forth and then got dumped onto the snowy ground when it came loose and broke. He was fine, he had not been high up on the vine, and the snow and undergrowth cushioned his landing. He laughed even harder and tossed snow into the air, hollering, "What a ride!"

After that, they picked up their burdens and headed back to the cabin happy about the day they had together. Without realizing it, they were becoming partners in their work and life. They were sharing and depending more and more on each other.

As the fire crackled in the fireplace one evening, they started talking about the woods and animals around them. Zeb told her the snow had a hard crust on it when he was out that sparkled like sunshine bouncing off the waves on a lake. It was crunching under his feet when he checked his traps that day, but he could walk on it with his snowshoes. He said many animals could just walk on top of it without leaving any tracks when it was thick like that. The deer had a hard time, though, because their sharp hooves would break through the crust with each step they took, and they would sink above their knees into deep snow that was under the crust. Sometimes the edges of the coating were so sharp they could even scrape their legs, and it slowed them down so much it was hard for them to get away from predators such as wolves. Something that nature made so beautiful and, pristine had a dark side too.

"Zeb, why do you live out here away from everyone?" Amelia asked him.

Zeb stopped what he was doing and stared off into the fire. He thought about her question for a while then answered her. "When I came to the woods, I found a deep calmness I had never felt before in my life. I did not have to live by anyone's rules and work from sunup to sundown for a boss. I was the boss, and what I did meant whether I ate or stayed warm or even survived. The world slowed down for me, and I started noticing little things I had taken for granted before. Things like how blue the shadows of a tree can be on white snow when the sun is shining. Other things as simple as all the different shapes and shades green moss can have, whether it is growing on a rock, or tree stump, or on the forest floor. Do you know when the ice starts melting on the lakes and ponds in spring, it makes loud booming noises? Almost as if it is talking to you, celebrating warm weather. And when the aspen trees shed their round yellow leaves in the wind, it looks like gold coins are drifting down around you?

When you go without food, or must work to get your own food, it tastes so much better. All my senses became more sharpened and tuned in to what was around me and I felt more alive than I had ever felt working in town in Rhode Island. I have even learned how to read tracks and tell what animal made them, what it was doing, where it came from, and where it was headed. One time I came across the print of what looked like outstretched angel wings in the snow, and I figured out an owl had swooped down and gotten a mouse there, leaving its wing prints when it lifted off.

The animals here kill for food to survive, not just because they have an argument or disagree with someone's beliefs. I respect them for that. Not like men. I killed a Redcoat when I was in the Rhode Island Militia. I did not even know his name or whether he had a family or not, and he did not know his killer. We were just enemies, strangers. With animals, I know their motives, how they have lived their lives, and what I am taking from them when I need to. Whether its deer, turkey, or fish, I appreciate what they give me.

Sometimes I come across something so beautiful that it seems out of place yet fits in perfectly like a patch of pink Moccasin Orchids growing in a shaded boggy area. Bridgette taught me the name of them. It is almost like God touched his finger right there in that spot, and something from the garden of Eden started growing. The smell of pines or sound of a small stream running down a waterfall is comforting and calming to me.

I am always learning more. Each time I am in the woods, I see or hear something I had not known before because it is ever-changing with the weather and seasons. I listen to the burst of different songs birds make in springtime and see all the types of nests they build. Or I hear a hawk calling to its mate as it rides the currents in the sky circling higher and higher. Sometimes I see something funny like a raccoon splashing water everywhere trying to catch a frog who keeps escaping, and it makes me laugh. I have watched a doe lick its spotted fawn's face clean like a mother washes her own child's face and seen young rabbits all snuggled together in a grassy nest. I know there is danger here with wild animals, such as bears and panthers. Even that fear makes me feel more alive. If they killed me, it would be for a good reason, and I would become part of their body and wild animal life. I would not have been killed just because someone did not believe in the same things I do. All I can say is I am living here, really living, I can feed myself and feed my soul, and I can breathe."

Amelia had listened, spellbound, to all that Zeb had been saying. For a man that had not talked to her much, he had just opened up entirely to her. What he said mirrored the way she felt about the woods and wild things, but she had never been able to put it into words like Zeb did. Zeb suddenly realized he had been talking for quite some time and stopped. He turned away and went back to what he had been doing.

He felt some purpose in his life again with Amelia and Kuskusky he had not felt for many months. They needed him for shelter and protection. Now that he was able to go out and trap again, he could also hunt and was getting venison and other game. He was out checking traps by himself one day and feeling lucky with his trapping season so far. He had some good-sized muskrats in his pack that day and was following his usual trail to check a trap he had set nearby. Earlier that week, while checking traps, he had seen some martin tracks in the snow and set one for that valuable fur animal.

He was pleased when he reached the set and saw he had caught a martin. Thinking it was dead, he reached in to get it, but the animal was still very much alive and only caught by one foot. It quickly whipped around and ripped into his hand several times with its razor-sharp teeth. Every curse he could think of flew out of his mouth before, bloodied and in pain, he quickly managed to end the animal's suffering. He did whatever he could to be sure the game he trapped swiftly died, but occasionally something like this martin's fate happened. The animal had gotten his revenge on Zeb, though. He held some packed snow on his hand to slow the bleeding, then wrapped it the best he could. He did not think the animal was rabid, it appeared healthy. It was in pain and fearful, so it tore into him more than once, just defending itself.

When he returned to the cabin, Amelia immediately noticed he had been injured. At first, Zeb brushed it off as nothing, but when he took the bloody wrapping off, she could see he had deep punctures, and his flesh was torn and gaping open. She got some herbs, ground them up and made a salve with honey and bee's wax. She held his hand tenderly as she cleaned the wounds. Then she used a sewing needle and some thread to stitch the gaps closed. Zeb watched her work silently as she cared for him. *She is a good woman*, he thought, *and it feels right to be close to her*. Amelia finished stitching his hand and then applied the salve and wrapped it.

"There, that should make it heal," she told Zeb.

He quietly thanked her. Their eyes lingered, looking at each other in unspoken affection for moments. He did not pull his hand from her gentle grip, and she did not let go. They both felt a stirring in their bodies they had not felt for a long time. Suddenly embarrassed by what she was feeling and realizing she had held his hand longer than she should, she let go and turned away.

After that day, Amelia noticed Zeb looking at her affectionately more than once. She was watching him also through the small window when he was working. She wanted to be closer to this strong but lonely man. Whenever she changed his dressing, their hands lingered longer than necessary before parting, and feelings of wanting to be closer were deepening.

On one sunny winter day, Kuskusky was being playful. Not sure if she wanted to be inside or out, she was going back and forth through the cabin door. Finally, she decided she wanted to climb a tree and be outdoors. The last time she went out, she had left the door slightly ajar. Amelia was busy at a small table laying out several pieces of bark and bundles of leaves she had collected and was getting them ready to dry. Zeb was on the other side of the room making repairs on a trap that was not working right. A sparrow flew through the door and then started circling the room, looking for a way out. Then it started hurling itself frantically against the window. It reminded Amelia of how she had felt at times. She was trapped, forced to winter in this cabin instead of living with the Cayuga where she wanted to be. Amelia stopped what she was doing to help the bird before it hurt itself. Each time she reached for it, the bird escaped her grasp and flew around the room, becoming even more agitated. Finally, it clung to a log in the corner of the ceiling, panting and looking frightened. It was out of her reach, though, so she asked Zeb for help to catch it.

He put down the trap he was working on and came to help her. Amelia stood on her toes and stretched to reach the bird, but she could not. Zeb was right behind her, and being taller, he came in close, reached over her head, and caught it in his hands. Amelia stepped backward, not realizing he was so close and leaned into his body before he could get out of the way. She fit perfectly against him. She was shocked at how it made her feel to have him press against her that way. She felt his body heat. It woke a longing within her for the closeness of a man. They gazed into each other's eyes for a moment, and then both embarrassed, they parted. Zeb took the sparrow to the door and released it. He did not say a word as he returned and glanced back at Amelia. She did not say anything either. Zeb went back to his traps, and Amelia let out a long, slow breath of air. It surprised her that Zeb was the man she now ached for.

Amelia tried not to be near Zeb after that day. Despite the feelings she had of wanting to be close to him, she was worried that he would send her and Kuskusky away at any time. She was not sure what this man thought of her or if she should trust her own feelings. There was another occasion that unsettled her. She had been picking up wood he was splitting by the chopping stump. Where they had walked, slippery snow was packed all around the area. She stepped close to where Zeb was working, slipped, and lost her footing. He reached out to catch her and hugged her close in his arms. Their faces were almost touching, and their eyes spoke the words their mouths had never formed. The world was closed off around them as he held her tight against him to keep her from falling. He leaned in and gently brushed his lips against her cheek and temple. His lips caressed her ear, and his hand slid down and felt her breast through her clothing. She closed her eyes and melted into him, but suddenly changed her mind, opened her eyes and angrily pushed him away. He let his arms fall to his side and lowered his head, sorry that he had lost control and taken such privileges. Once again, the spell was broken, they separated and glanced at each other at arm's length without saying a word. Reluctantly, they continued with the chores they were doing.

Both were unsettled by the emotions and need they felt when they held each other so close. Amelia was conflicted about what was happening to her. She did not belong with this trapper. She had plans to travel to the place of the Great Council Fire and start a new home for her daughter there. But she felt so alone since she had lost Tamataunee and her people. When Zeb had held her in his arms, she felt sheltered and protected and, even more unsettling, she felt wanted. *He is lonely and hurting too,* she thought. *We could comfort each other if only for a short while. Should I turn away from that?*

One evening Kuskusky had fallen asleep in her little bed and Amelia had laid down on the warm furs on the floor as usual. The snow was falling gently outside. The candles were out in the cabin, and the only light was the golden glow of the burning logs. Amelia looked across the room to where Zeb lay. He was gazing warmly back at her.

Without saying anything, he patted the bed beside him, folded back the quilt, and motioned for her to join him. She ached so much to be close to him, to feel his arms encircling her. She checked on Kuskusky, who was sleeping soundly, then rose slowly and walked softly across the room. Standing beside his bed, she pulled her dress over her head, let it drop to the floor and stepped out of it. She stood there naked before him and could feel his eyes study her body. Then he reached out for her hand and gently pulled her into his bed. He covered her tenderly with his quilt then wrapped his arms around her as he kissed her neck and felt her bare skin touching his. This time she did not stop him when his hands sought her body. Neither of them stopped nor parted. They were careful in their passion discovering the heat of each other not to wake the sleeping child. All fear for the future, all sadness and worry were consumed in the furnace of their physical fire. Time and thoughts paused as they melted and merged like molten metal one into the other.

CHAPTER 6

AFTER THAT EVENING, THEIR LIVES TOGETHER changed a great deal. They stopped just coexisting and became partners, sharing each other's lives and caring about each other's needs. Zeb spent extra time talking and playing with Kuskusky, who was now almost four years old. He played checkers with her, letting her win, of course, and held her hand often when they were on walks. He would set her on his knees as they listened to the Lenape stories Amelia told in the evenings. He was also teaching her about the animals and their tracks and habits in the woods. He especially enjoyed having Amelia in his warm embrace each night.

One evening he surprised Amelia and Kuskusky when he got a harmonica out and started playing it. His first song was "Baa Baa Black Sheep," which Amelia recognized from her own childhood and sang it to Kuskusky, who thought it was very funny, clapped her hands, and made Zeb play it again. The second song he played before he stopped was "Amazing Grace." That song also brought back memories for Amelia and made her long to see her parents again. When Zeb played the verse "I once was lost, but now I am found," it had new meaning for them both.

Several weeks passed and it started to show signs of a sunny spring. The days were getting longer and not so bitter cold. When the temperature rose above freezing during the day, then plunged to freezing at night, the difference would prime the fluid in the trees. Sap would move back up from its winter rest in the roots, and its vitality would flow back into the limbs. It was the time of the maples and making maple sugar. Amelia noticed signs of sap returning to the branches by seeing streaks of wet bark where a tree had been injured, so she knew the maples were coming alive. Woodpeckers took advantage of any opportunity to get the sap by licking up little trickles coming from where they had pecked holes on the maples. It was a sure sign it was early spring and time to tap the maple trees.

Amelia made some bark containers to catch the sap, and Zeb listened and followed her directions on how to cut a V on the maple tree and drive in a stick with a narrow channel below it. The Lenape had been making maple sugar for many years. Amelia had done it with her family several times, but Zeb had no experience maple sugaring. Amelia told Zeb she needed a wooden paddle for stirring the sap, and he carved one that was perfect for keeping the boiling fluid from scorching. He also followed her directions to carve a wooden bowl from basswood for working the maple sugar. They set up a large metal pot outdoors and kept the fire going as they boiled the sap down into syrup. When the syrup got thick and turned into a beautiful amber color, Amelia put it into the wooden bowl to crystalize. She stirred in some deer tallow to keep the sugar crystals soft. When it became cool enough, she worked it first with a wooden paddle and then with her hands to break it up into granulated maple sugar. Then she stored it in some birch bark containers. She could make storage baskets from other kinds of trees, but the properties of birch bark kept food from spoiling, so it was the best to use for the precious maple sugar. Soon, the leaf buds on the trees burst open and reddish leaves started to emerge. The sap stopped flowing and the time of the maples ended.

Here and there, pockets of aged snow could still be seen littering the woods where it had drifted up high or where piles had escaped the warmth of the spring sun. Now, there was green moss, dark earth, and patches of umbrella-like ground pine showing in the woods. Amelia thought about continuing her journey to the Cayuga and wondered if she should leave before Zeb forced her to go. She was not sure how he felt about her even though they had become so close over the winter. He was resuming more of his trapping activities and left for long periods. Did he stay away because he had to, or did he want to distance himself from them? Amelia and Kuskusky could be happy living with Zeb. However, he seemed to prefer a solitary life. Amelia still felt it would be best for her to live with the Cayuga.

The day was bright and warm with a clear, cerulean blue sky and the smell of new growth. Birds were active, pulling out blades of dry grasses for making nests, calling to each other and defending their territories. Amelia decided she would go to the beaver pond to catch some fish. They had not had fish in some time, and it would be a welcome change. She told Kuskusky to get ready, then got her fishing pole and set off for the pond. It was swampy all around the pond, which had grown from the melt of snow, plus the beaver had expanded its dam. Amelia found a place where Kuskusky could be close to her while she fished. Fish were rising to feed on bugs hovering over the surface of the pond, and scores of bugs were hatching from the water's surface as well. The hungry fish were leaving big circles as they gulped down the hatch of insects. That was a good sign to her that fishing might be productive that day. Zeb had given Amelia a couple good metal hooks for fishing, and she found some bait, put it on, and cast her line out into the pond.

Standing there in the warmth of the day, she felt a bug biting the back of her uncovered arm and swatted it away. Soon many mosquitos started biting her all over. When she heard Kuskusky start crying, she knew she was getting bitten as well. She saw a swarm all around her little girl who was frantically trying to swat them away. Amelia threw her fishing pole down and ran to help her. The vampires soon became a black cloud of biting, buzzing bugs circling and attacking them both, and Amelia quickly grabbed Kuskusky to take her away from there. Amelia was getting viciously bitten around her face, neck, and on her arms and legs where her clothing did not cover her skin. They were even biting her around her eyes. Some bites were bloody holes in her skin, and she did her best to swat the hungry parasites as soon as she felt their sting, but her biggest concern was protecting Kuskusky. She broke off a leafy branch to brush the bugs away from Kuskusky, but was it enough? She hoped Kuskusky was not getting bitten like she was. The swarm followed them for some time as they were escaping, all the while biting Amelia as she hurried away. Once they were further into the cool woods away from the water, the mosquitos finally left them alone.

As soon as she returned to the safety of the cabin, she checked Kuskusky for any bites. Luckily, she did not have many as she feared. Amelia crushed the bulbs of some leeks and applied them to the bites she found on Kuskusky, who said it took the hurt away. Once she had treated Kuskusky, she started treating the areas where she had been bitten. There were a lot of them. Her skin was itching and burning with red raised bumps all over. She applied some crushed leeks to her bites also, and soon they felt less irritated and itchy. "There will be no fish for us today Kuskusky," she told her daughter, "instead the bugs fed on us. Next time I will be prepared, and we will put some grease on our skins to keep the biting bugs away." Amelia was thankful Kuskusky had not been bitten as bad as she had been.

Days after that, Amelia felt faint and dizzy and started to get a fever. Zeb had returned from his trapping and was stretching pelts onto frames when he noticed she appeared flushed. Soon she told him she needed to lay down and asked him to watch Kuskusky while she rested for a short while. However, her short rest became much longer. Zeb saw how flushed her face was, went to her side, and felt her head and cheeks. Instantly he was concerned, she was burning up with fever. When he asked her what was wrong, she acted confused and had trouble telling him how she felt. He brought her some water and urged her to sip it. But he did not know how else to help her. He asked if she had some medicine he could get for her, but by then, she was delirious and incoherent. Without her telling him what to do, he was helpless to do anything. He had heard of fevers that came on suddenly and kept getting worse until a person died.

He was so concerned about her but had no idea how to help except give her water. Soon she was sleeping so much, getting her to swallow was challenging to do. He put cold, wet cloth on her forehead and sat down beside her. She had saved his life, and he had grown to love her as a woman, friend, and mother who doted on her little girl with all the love she could show her. He owed her so much. She had literally saved him from dying a terrible death. He owed her all he could do to help her through this sickness. Then he wondered how he should care for Kuskusky? Amelia had always taken care of whatever the little girl needed. He was trying to remember what he had seen her do at the cabin to care for the child. Should I fix her something to eat now? In his worry and fear for Amelia, he was confused about caring for the little child and Amelia. I cannot leave Amelia to travel and get help, and I cannot take her with me either in her condition. He prayed God would not take the Lenape woman from her child and from him.

Amelia lay in bed for several days going in and out of consciousness while still running a high fever. She was getting weaker every day. Zeb kept placing cold, wet cloths on her head, but there was nothing else he could think of to help her through this sickness. He told himself, if only she could tell me what medicines I could give her, there is probably something right here that she gathered. However, Amelia could not give him those instructions. As the days went by, he became sure she was going to die. He also prayed Kuskusky and him would not get sick with whatever was wrong with her. "Amelia, you must get better," he told her. "We need you; I cannot take this little girl out trapping with me." He was already considering the sad possibility that he would have to bury Amelia. He was sitting in a chair beside her bed, completely worn out from worry and feeling so helpless as she wasted away. Then he heard someone call out from the area in front of the cabin.

"Hello! Hello, owner of this cabin, is anyone here?"

Zeb rose from the chair and peered out his small window and saw a couple on horses. The man wore a black coat and black shirt with a white collar around his neck. The woman wore a long dark dress, coat, and hat and seemed out of place sitting on the horse.

"Hello, is anyone home?" he called out again.

Zeb went to the door and opened it slowly, his rifle was hanging right over the entrance in case he needed it. He thought these visitors did not look like they were dangerous. Out here in this wilderness, though, many dishonest people were passing themselves off as friends. He took the rifle down and set it just inside the doorjamb where it would be handy and stepped outside and pulled the door partially closed. Any prying eyes could not see the sick woman and child inside.

"I am here, and who are you?" he asked the two strangers.

"Hello, sir. I am Reverend Abraham Vickery, pleased to meet you, and this is my wife, Hestor. We are traveling around the territory of our new church. We have received a commandment to go forth and teach the word to any that will listen. However, we have strayed off our path and need directions to return to our mission in Kanadesaga. We saw the smoke from your chimney at a distance, which led us here. Good man, can we talk for a short while before you show us the way we need to return?"

Zeb thought about the two sitting there on horseback for a moment, he was still angry at God for taking his wife Bridgette and did not want to be preached to or argue religion with anyone. The man seemed friendly as he clutched his bible and talked to Zeb. His wife smiled at him warmly, and Zeb suddenly realized she might be someone who could help with Amelia. He explained to them both that Amelia was extremely ill, and he did not know what was wrong with her.

Then facing the preacher's wife, he asked her, "Could you please come take a look at my woman, I do not know what is wrong, and I am worried."

The woman cautiously asked, "Does she have any blisters or red rash on her? That would be a medical condition we do not want to get near."

"No, it is nothing like that. I do not think it is infectious because I would be sick by now. She has been ill for several days. Please, come in and look at her."

The Reverend's wife stepped down from her horse and came into the cabin while her husband got the reins and took both horses over and tied them to a tree. Hestor went to Amelia's side as soon as she entered the cabin. She felt Amelia's head and lifted a closed eyelid to look at her eyes. She examined her gums and felt her hands and feet, then listened to her breathing.

Then, standing up, she asked Zeb, "How long has she been like this?"

"For well over a week now," he answered.

"Has she been running a high fever most of that time?" Hestor asked.

"Yes, she has, and she is sleeping most of the time and not eating. She just swallows a little water occasionally. She talks crazy sometimes too and then passes back out." Frustrated and worried, Zeb asked her, "Can you help her; can you tell me what is wrong?"

Hestor was shaking her head slowly back and forth. "I have seen this before. It is called Swamp Fever. They think it is from the bad air around the wet areas."

The Reverend joined them and spoke up. "Leeches are good for many ailments and might help if you could get some for her." He added, "The blood can become quite impure, and bloodletting by leeches cleanses it."

"Oh, no!" Hestor told him, "They are disgusting and nasty. I would never use such ugly creatures for healing. You must give her lots of water, as much as she will take. Force it on her if you must. Do you have any medicines here? I learned how to use native medicines in my training."

Zeb showed her all the different bundles and pouches of healing and cooking herbs Amelia had gathered. Hestor could see dried plants hanging from rafters and in little pouches and baskets around the room. She started going through the bundles of dried plants and rubbed and sniffed leaves until she recognized some. Zeb did not know one plant from another. He had no idea whether the herbs were used for cooking or for healing. Fortunately, Hestor could identify catnip, tansy, plantain, and mountain mint, which were medicinal herbs for fevers and diseases. She gave handfuls of them to Zeb and told him to make a tea of them, let it cool a little, and give it to Amelia as often as he could make her drink it. It would drive the sickness out of her.

Sadly, not wanting to say the words, Zeb asked, "Is she going to live?"

"That is up to God, young man." Hestor told him, "We will pray for her, but this squaw is exceedingly sick, and she is so low on energy now it is hard to say. You will know in a few days. If she does survive, it will take a long time for her to be strong again. It is a wasting disease that some never fully recover from. But do not give up hope, there is always the chance of a miracle." Then, looking around the room, she noticed Kuskusky sitting on the floor playing with her little cattail doll. "Is she an Indian child?" she asked in a concerned voice.

"Yes, she is Amelia's child. I believe she is Seneca. She is a sweet little girl; I do not know what I will do if Amelia does not recover. I cannot take care of a small child like her and do my trapping too." Zeb was shaken by the thought of losing someone else in his life he genuinely cared for.

Hestor stared at Kuskusky, shaking her head. "That little girl needs cleaning up right now. When was the last time she had something to eat?"

Zeb tried to think. Had he remembered to give her some food, and when might that have been? He had been so concerned about Amelia, he was not paying attention to Kuskusky and was not sure. "I think I gave her something a little while ago."

Reverend Vickery was leaning over Amelia with his bible in his hands. "This Indian squaw should be baptized so she can get into heaven," he told Zeb.

Zeb thought about the Reverend's words. "I am not sure she wants that. She follows the beliefs of her people. She may have already been baptized when she was younger. Besides, I wonder sometimes if her native Creator God is not the same being as our Creator God."

Reverend Vickery and Hestor were both shocked at his remark. "I am aware of the native's heathen beliefs. Sadly, they are so unschooled in spiritual matters. That is why we are here preaching to them in the hope that we may enlighten them. We have a small mission near Kanadesaga and are making some progress in converting them," Reverend Vickery told him.

"Amelia said the colonial army had destroyed many Seneca villages. Was the village of Kanadesaga attacked too?" Zeb asked.

"General Sullivan and his army destroyed every Seneca village all the way up to Geneva. They burned their crops and girdled their orchards so the trees would die. Game is much scarcer now too, and the natives that survived are dependent on us to help them live." Reverend Vickery told Zeb.

"That is too bad. I traded with a few, and I never had a problem." Zeb explained where Thanaowyte's village had been and asked if they knew what had happened to it. They told him every Seneca village was destroyed along the shoreline of Seneca Lake all the way to the top of the lake. Not one had been spared.

His wife, Hestor, was at Kuskusky's side and was stroking her hair and patting her on her back. "You should let us take this little Indian girl until her mother gets well enough to care for her again. We will undoubtedly clean her up and feed and take care of her properly. We will give her some schooling too while she is with us. We can take her back with us to Kanadesaga to stay with us for a short while. You can come to get her when you are ready. If this squaw does not survive, well, that would be very sad, but the child would be in a good place to be taken care of."

Zeb thought about Hestor's advice. Amelia lay on the bed so feverish and unconscious most of the time. *How much longer could she last like this?* He wondered. *She was so pale now and losing weight. What if she does not live?* He looked over at Kuskusky and knew he could not take as good care of her. Hestor's offer made a lot of sense. She needed a woman's nurturing, not a rough trapper like him. It was a hard, unfair decision to make, but reluctantly he agreed to let them take Kuskusky with them when they left. Zeb knew where the Seneca village of Kanadesaga was and could get Kuskusky back anytime.

They all gathered around Amelia lying on the bed, and the Reverend said a prayer. Hestor reminded Zeb to keep forcing her to drink water and broth and use the herbs. Zeb gave them good directions to Kanadesaga, and then they left, taking Kuskusky and some of her meager belongings with them. Before she left, she ran over to Amelia's side and placed her small cattail doll next to her.

She looked up at Zeb, "Momma's does not feel good." Then she turned to go with Hestor. She started crying a little and stared back at Zeb when she was going out the door, but they got her interested in riding the horse with Hestor holding onto her, and she calmed down.

Zeb told Kuskusky he would come and get her soon as he waved goodbye and watched them leave. Then he re-entered the cabin and closed the door behind him. The cabin suddenly felt empty to him with Kuskusky gone. He had gotten used to her being around and enjoyed hearing her laughter and chatter. Zeb wondered, what would Amelia do when she found out her daughter had been taken away? The preacher and his wife had convinced him that was the best thing to do. Kuskusky would be alright for a short time with those people, he told himself. *I will bring her back.*

Amelia stirred, and he went to her side. She was feverish again and seemed to be having a nightmare. She called out Tamataunee's name. He wet another cloth and put it on her head to calm her. He studied the features of her face as he sat by her bed. He loved her dark braided hair. She spent so much time working outdoors; her complexion was tanned and dark like the Lenape and Seneca. With her beaded and colorfully stitched clothing, it was easy to mistake her for a full-blooded native. But looking closely, you could tell she was a colonial woman by heritage, and a beautiful one, he thought. He picked up her hand and laid it gently in his big one. She had gotten callouses from helping him split and pile wood as well as all the other hard chores she did for them. Zeb knew so little about her. He had never taken the time to find out anything about her life before he met her. Have you suffered Amelia? He thought about how she had taken care of him when he was bedridden with broken legs.

Amelia had been patient while he had been angry and impatient. She had taken care of him and Kuskusky and cooked and kept the cabin clean plus killed some game for them to eat. He realized he cared deeply for this woman and would feel tremendous grief if he lost her to this wasting disease. He kept a close vigil by her side for several days, forcing her to drink whenever she was alert enough and spooning some soup into her when she would take it. Finally, the fever broke, and her temperature lowered.

Although she was terribly weak and trembling, she tried to sit up and speak to him. "What has happened?" Were her first words, immediately followed by, "Kuskusky, come to mother."

CHAPTER 7

"**Y**OU HAVE BEEN AWFULLY SICK FOR days and days," Zeb told her as he encouraged her to lie back. There was no resistance from her as he pushed her gently on her shoulders. He pulled the covers up around her and adjusted her pillow. "You need to keep drinking water. You have had a high fever for too long." Zeb got water in a tin cup and gently cradled her head as she sipped a little, and then overcome by weakness, she fell back to sleep. Zeb felt hopeful; Amelia might come through this crisis, but she was far from being out of danger. *She is so frail, not the strong, independent woman she had been. I wonder if she will be the same Amelia I knew, or will she become an invalid?*

When she called out for Kuskusky the next time, Zeb told her about Hestor, the older woman who offered to take care of her daughter for a short while.

"Amelia, when you are well enough, I will bring her back to you."

Amelia was so distressed to find out Kuskusky was gone. She felt somewhat relieved Kuskusky was being cared for by a woman but wanted her near so she could see and touch her daughter and make sure her needs were being met. It took weeks before Amelia could get out of bed and walk on her own without feeling so weak that she had to suddenly sit down. Amelia asked Zeb several times to go get Kuskusky, but he told her she was too weak for the journey yet, and he did not want to leave her alone. Recurring fevers and dizziness still racked her at times and set her progress back. Weeks became a couple months, and finally, she regained some strength, and there were no more relapses. Amelia was now strong enough to travel and get her daughter.

Zeb and Amelia packed what they needed for traveling. He checked his gunpowder, cleaned his gun, and was ready for any problems with animals, the French, or anything that might interfere with their task. They rolled up a blanket for resting on the ground at night. Zeb had told her it was a couple of nights walk to Kanadesaga, where Kuskusky was staying at the mission. Amelia assured him she could walk that far and back now. She would walk any distance to hold her daughter again. While she was recuperating, she had made a pair of moccasins for Kuskusky and decorated them with beads taken from her own clothing. They left early and struck out toward the big lake. Zeb traded with Seneca near the top of the lake and knew the way. They did not stop often; Amelia was anxious to see Kuskusky and wanted to push right through. Zeb forced her to travel at a slower pace, however, and take short rests so she would not get overtired. She had been through so much. This trip could make her ill again if they were not careful.

When they occasionally rested, he asked about her earlier life. Zeb wanted to know how she came to live with the natives. He also told her of his life with Bridgette and her sad, unexpected passing. Amelia finally understood why he had been so depressed and unhappy when she first came to his cabin.

They pushed on and arrived on the outskirts of Kanadesaga. It was just a small cluster of buildings. Zeb pointed out one home with a cross on it that he thought was the home of Reverend Vickery and his wife. A white picket fence enclosed the front yard, and he pushed open the gate and walked up the dirt path. Zeb knocked on the door and was greeted by a young Seneca girl dressed in a grey shift dress. She kept her eyes downward, and her manner was so quiet and subdued for a child her age. Amelia was surprised to see that her dark hair had been cut into a short bob hairstyle, unlike the way the Seneca usually wore theirs. He asked to speak to the Reverend and was told, "I am sorry, sir, he is not here now."

A voice called out to the young girl from another room. "Patience, who is at the door?" a woman asked, "Show them in here, girl."

Zeb and Amelia anxiously entered the hallway and were led to a room where three women were gathered doing embroidery on hoops of cloth they were holding. They saw Kuskusky standing off to the side of the room, and when she saw Amelia, she rushed forward to her outstretched arms.

Hestor caught her by the shoulder before she had taken a few steps forward and reprimanded her saying, "Catherine, mind your manners. Young ladies do not rush at people when they see them." Hestor let go of her, and Kuskusky slowly approached Amelia, then hugged her tightly.

"Oh, that is sweet," one of the other ladies remarked.

Hestor smiled and told her, "Catherine, you must curtsy when you meet an older woman." Kuskusky's shoulders slumped, she let go of Amelia and then curtsied in front of her. Mother and daughter both had tear-filled eyes. Amelia gave Kuskusky her small cattail doll, and she smiled and hugged it.

"Can you see what fine manners your young girl has learned here?" Hestor asked, beaming, "and we call her Catherine now, it is much more civilized than Kuskusky. Soon the whole area around Seneca Lake will be settled by new people. There are merchants, farmers, and shop-keepers coming this way to homestead, and they will need help. She must have proper manners and an English name if she wants to work in a good house."

"What do you mean work in a good house?" Zeb asked.

"Why to get employment as a servant girl, what else did you expect for an Indian?" Hestor said, raising her eyebrows. "The Indian villages are gone. The land is ours now, rightfully given to us by our government, and everything around has become the Military Tract. Soldiers are coming back and claiming land for themselves. Look at our little town here, how fast it is growing with new homes being built. Catherine will be needed to work in one of them, and it would be good for her. She would live in a civilized house and have regular meals."

"We want to take her back home with us now where she should be. She has a home and would get regular meals." Amelia said. She stepped forward and pulled Kuskusky close to her.

Hestor stood. "I saw how she was being neglected when I was at that crude cabin of yours. No, that is not what is best for her. You should leave this young girl here. We can raise her properly. We have other Indian children living here with us learning to overcome their native ways." Hestor waved her hand, "Patience, come here." The Indian girl who answered the door approached Hestor. "Would you freshen our tea please, Patience, our cups are almost empty."

With that request, Patience curtsied and said, "Yes, Ma'am." Then she walked to the table, took the cozy off the teapot, and approached the women gathered there one at a time to pour tea. The ladies held out their porcelain cups and nodded while smiling at Zeb and Amelia, confirming their approval of how Patience served them.

"See, Catherine will do that soon too. Right now, we have been so busy trying to teach her basic manners. Do you know she would prefer to go barefoot and splash in puddles than wear shoes like a decent young lady? Last week she even caught a toad by the woodpile. She held it in her hands, playing with it. It is a wonder she does not have warts all over her body, the foolish child. I have had to discipline her more than once for tricks like that." Hestor was shaking her head. "I have had to teach her so much! Sometimes I wonder if she is not just simple-minded. She does not know how to wash clothes or read her verses properly, and her manners are atrocious. She often forgets to say, ‹Yes, Mrs. Vickery and no, Mrs. Vickery.' She needs to learn civilized manners, and she will not get that from you. Also, the child lies! She told me a crazy story about little people living in the woods. I am afraid if she goes back to that crude cabin of yours, she will forget what we have taught her and lose all the progress we have made." Hestor sucked in her breath and elevated her nose as she glared at Zeb and Amelia.

The other ladies were all shaking their heads 'yes' in agreement. One of them remarked, "It would be a shame for Catherine to forget all Mrs. Vickery has taught her."

"But she is my daughter," Amelia told her, pleading, "I cannot leave her here; I miss her terribly and want her to come back home with us."

Hestor showed none of the friendliness or kindness Zeb had seen at his cabin when Amelia was ill. Then tight mouthed she said firmly, "That would be a grave mistake, I do not think I can let you do that." Alarmed by those words, Amelia's eyes widened, and she studied the stern faces staring at them.

Zeb spoke up, "You promised me Kuskusky could stay with you for a short time only while Amelia was so gravely ill. It is time for her to come home now, she is going back with us."

Hestor crossed her arms and rocked back on her heels. She raised her voice and loudly told him, "That was weeks and weeks ago, sir. Now that I know how much schooling and manners this child needs to learn; I firmly believe she must stay here. I cannot let you take her."

With that, she reached forward and tried to pull Kuskusky back from Amelia, who loudly told her, "No, you cannot keep her."

Hestor and Amelia were both shouting and Kuskusky was crying when Reverend Vickery, with his bodyguard, rushed into the room. The guard had a gun in his hand and pointed it at Zeb and Amelia. The ladies all suddenly stood up in fear and clustered together.

"What is the problem here?" the Reverend asked his wife.

"They want to take Catherine back to that awful cabin," Hestor told him, disgusted, "tell them they cannot do that!"

Reverend Vickery pointed his finger straight at Zeb and Amelia and told them, "You people need to leave my home now, and Catherine stays here, she will be fine with us and has been happy until she saw you both. We will teach her to be a child with duty, reverence, and polite manners to her elders."

Everyone fell silent with the new danger of a gun in the room. Zeb looked at Hestor and the Reverend, then back at the guard, and saw the determination on their faces and the weapon. The Reverend tugged on Kuskusky by the arm and tried to pull her from Amelia, who would not let go.

Zeb whispered in her ear, "Let Kuskusky go, for now, we will get her another time." Tension crackled in the air. Reluctantly Amelia let loose of Kuskusky, and the Reverend pulled her away towards Hestor.

"Catherine, go stand by Mrs. Vickery," the Reverend barked out the order while firmly pointing to where he wanted her to stand. She fearfully went and stood by Hestor.

Hestor gripped Kuskusky tightly by her hand, "Stop that foolish sniveling!" She said as she took the cattail doll from her and flung it towards a nearby chair where it bounced off and fell to the floor.

"Now go on, get out of here," the Reverend told Zeb and Amelia, motioning them towards the door. They left the room with the guard following close behind to make sure they obeyed.

Amelia was so upset as Zeb led her back down the path and out through the gate. She tried to turn back, saying, "Zeb, I cannot leave her there."

But Zeb pulled her forward and told her quietly, "Do not worry, we will get her back soon. We must plan how to do that." The guard stood at the doorway with his gun ready, watching them leave. They left the settlement and went into the woods nearby. Once they were some distance into the cover of the woods, Zeb stopped and started setting up a camp.

"What are you doing?" Amelia asked as she broke down entirely and sobbed. "We have to go back and get Kuskusky now."

Zeb put his arms around her to calm her crying and told her, "We will, but we have to plan it carefully, Amelia, or we may both get hurt. If we do not do this right, we could get shot, then they would keep Kuskusky forever. You do not want that to happen, do you?"

"No," was all Amelia could reply between her sobs as she shook her head.

Zeb held her by the shoulders and looked into her face. "Listen to me Amelia, we are going to watch the house and their daily activities to see a time Kuskusky is unguarded. We will take her away from them and leave before they notice. We will camp here for the night and tomorrow I will watch the house. They must let her come out sometime during the day. Remember, Hestor told us Kuskusky wanted to take her shoes off and run barefoot outdoors?"

"Yes, she did say that," Amelia answered softly.

"People like Hestor and Reverend Vickery do the same things day after day. They are like an animal who wakes at the same time and looks for food on the same trail. I will watch the house and see when Kuskusky is outdoors. I will get her back with us, Amelia, I promise." Zeb told her. "Now rest, you have had a long journey, and we have more to do. We need to rest and be strong for what is ahead of us." Zeb spread out the blanket they had brought, led Amelia over to it, and encouraged her to lie down. He lay down beside her, and she fell asleep, still letting out a sob now and then as she dreamed of her daughter.

When daylight broke, Zeb told her to stay there and he would sneak back and watch the house to see what they did that day. Reluctantly, Amelia agreed to wait there. When he reached Hestor's home, he found a place out of sight behind some brush and kept watch for any movements in and out of the household. The first person he saw was the older Indian girl, Patience, coming out a door on the small wing and going out back to the chicken house. Shortly after, with her basket full of eggs, she went back into the house. Zeb was sure that was the kitchen wing because a chimney was sending up smoke from a stove. It was a small home with glass-paned windows hung with curtains, so it was difficult to see into the interior.

In the late morning, he saw Patience and Kuskusky come out the same door carrying a heavy wicker basket of laundry. They sat it down by the clothesline that ran from the side of the house to a tree. Kuskusky reached into the basket and handed a garment to Patience, who took it from her, shook it out, and pinned it to the clothesline. They had several clothes hung up when Mrs. Vickery came storming out the door, slammed it behind her, and shouted at them. She had a willow switch, and went to Patience, grabbed her roughly by the shoulder and whipped the back of her legs with the switch. Then she told Kuskusky to turn around and used the switch to whip her legs as well.

Hestor took a pair of men's pants off the line, shook them at Patience telling her she hung them upside down on the clothesline, and that was not the way she had been taught. Zeb could tell Kuskusky and Patience were both cowering in fear of the angry woman standing over them.

He heard Hestor say loudly. "Now, do it the way I showed you!"

Patience quickly took the pair of pants and hung them up the way Hestor wanted. Satisfied, Hestor scowled and pointed her finger at them, both saying, "Well, I hope you learned your lesson. Tell me you are sorry!"

Both girls lowered their heads and answered her with, "I am sorry, Mrs. Vickery." Finished with her wrath, she went back into the house, again slamming the door behind her.

Patience and Kuskusky silently stared at each other and then quietly continued their work. Zeb wanted so much to just rush over and snatch her away right then, but if Mrs. Vickery had noticed Patience hanging the pants up wrong, she was probably closely watching the girls. He did not know where the Reverend and his guard were, so he stayed rooted where he was out of sight. They are using those girls as slaves, he thought. No wonder they do not want to give Kuskusky back. Later in the day, he saw the girls outside again. This time Patience was splitting firewood, and Kuskusky was stacking it. When they finished, they both carried wood inside for the kitchen stove and fireplaces. Kuskusky was struggling to walk under the load of wood she was carrying. Zeb's heart went out to her, and he felt the urge again to rush in and take her away, but it was not a safe time to do that. He had not seen the Reverend, or his guard leave the house and was not sure what they were doing right then. Later, when Zeb returned to their camp, Amelia was waiting anxiously to see her daughter.

"You did not bring her!" she cried out when she saw he was alone.

"Not this time Amelia, but I will soon." He told her what he had seen that day, and Amelia was upset about how Kuskusky was being treated. "She is a strong little girl Amelia. She has the blood of her ancestors in her, just like you told her when she was with us. We will get her back from them. I promise you."

"But I want to get her away from them now," Amelia said, pleading.

"We need to have a plan and do it when it is safe for her. I think we should watch the house more and take her back when the Reverend and his guard are away, and Hestor is not watching her so closely. Tomorrow I will watch their activities, so I know what they do each day."

He and Amelia spent another restless night together. The next morning Zeb went back to the house and hid out of sight again. Later in the morning, he noticed the guard arrive, and he went into the residence. Shortly after that, the Reverend and his guard came out, mounted their horses and left. Good, Zeb thought, now I must know what Hestor is doing. He kept a close eye on the home. Not much was happening, and then he saw the girls leave the house to get firewood again.

The older girl was splitting wood as she had done before, and Kuskusky was stacking it. As he watched them, he saw two women come to the front door. Hestor was greeting them and inviting them to go inside. *This is my chance*, he quickly realized and rushed to the back of the home to get Kuskusky. He startled her at first, but when she recognized him, she threw her arms around him and held on tight. Zeb held his finger to his lips, motioning both girls to be silent. Without saying a word, he picked her up and rushed her away out of sight. Patience stood right where she was with the ax at her side and watched Zeb and Kuskusky leaving. She glanced warily at the back door, but she did not say a word as Zeb left with Kuskusky. She realized it was a rescue and wished she was being taken from that place as well. Zeb hoped Hestor would not punish the girl for not warning her that Kuskusky was escaping. Zeb and Kuskusky were quickly on their way to the place where Amelia was waiting.

When he arrived with Kuskusky, Amelia was so happy to see her daughter; she hugged her tightly, stroked her hair lovingly, and comforted her.

"You are safe now with mother, Kuskusky," she told her. It saddened her to see that Kuskusky was no longer her bubbly, happy little girl. Now she had a sadness about her and was very quiet. *I hope her soul can return to the happiness she had before they took her from me*, Amelia silently prayed.

Zeb put his hand on her shoulder and spoke up, "Amelia, we cannot stay here any longer. Reverend Vickery and his guard are on horseback, and we are on foot. I do not know where they are right now, but if they try to find us, they can travel faster than we can. We need to go now before Hestor realizes Kuskusky is gone and alerts anyone. They will come searching for us soon."

Amelia helped Zeb pack up what they had brought, and they struck out toward his cabin as fast as they could walk. They rested only briefly on the way, and Zeb was sure to cover what tracks he could or leave a confusing false direction track now and then just in case they were being hunted.

Amelia held Kuskusky's hand as they walked. She had grown up so much during Ahmeya's terrible illness and her captivity and was a strong little girl now like her mother had been at her age. Zeb urged them all to be silent and not make any sounds that someone might hear to detect their presence. Once they were deep into the woods and had stopped for the night, he started talking.

"Amelia, when we get back to our cabin, we will pack up the furs I have and take them to Newtown. I do not want to be at the cabin if anyone comes looking for Kuskusky to take her back. The Reverend might remember where our cabin is. They might even try to kidnap her sometime when we are not watching her closely, just like I did."

Hearing that, Kuskusky pleaded, "Mother, do not let them take me away again."

"Kuskusky, you are staying right here with me. No one will take you away again." she told her daughter. "Zeb, can't we just tell them they cannot have her and fight them?" Amelia asked.

"I wish it were that simple Amelia, but it is not. The Reverend is considered an authority here. If you argue too much or point a gun at them, you will give them a reason to hurt you and do what they want. They will say you are a hostile. You are considered an Indian squaw with Kuskusky as your child. They will think I am not suitable living with you as my wife also, and that I am uncivilized and undeserving of raising Kuskusky. Reverend Vickery and Hestor want to take her because they think they are better than us and can give her what they call a civilized life." Zeb paused, and with his hands on his hips, he shook his head and talked in a lowered voice. "No, we cannot fight them, Amelia. We must get away from them. It is not enough to be brave and defiant against that kind of person. Even if we could send the Reverend and his guard away, there are more men in that settlement. They would come back. If a powerful, dangerous mountain lion is roaming your territory and you cannot kill him, you need to get a new territory, or he will hunt and kill you."

Amelia sadly agreed with him. They slept only briefly that night, and before daylight, they were traveling home. Once they arrived at their cabin, Zeb told them both to the only pack what was necessary.

"We must hurry. I have a place where I have hidden a canoe along the shore of Seneca Lake. We will use that and travel down the lake to Newtown, and I will sell my furs to the buyer there."

Kuskusky happily took her grey linsey-woolsey shift off and put on her soft suede deerskin dress. Now she felt like an Indian child again. Although Amelia wore colorful cotton clothing now, she made Kuskusky a sturdy deerskin dress because her little girl was such an outdoor child climbing trees and exploring the woods. Amelia packed some foodstuffs and what essentials she could into a woven backpack she made so long ago. Checking around, she noticed the bible with the drawings tucked inside and slid that into her backpack also. Kuskusky could learn to read verses from it.

Zeb was busy loading his large backpack with traps and all the furs he could roll up tight. He had too many and asked Amelia, "Do you think Kuskusky could carry some of these?" as he held out some ermine and mink pelts.

"Yes, I can," Kuskusky answered firmly before Amelia said anything. "I am a Seneca daughter, and I know how to carry burdens."

Zeb and Amelia both smiled at each other. They saw a spark of what Kuskusky used to be. Zeb tied a smaller bundle of furs together for her. Amelia quickly fashioned straps so Kuskusky could carry it on her back. Zeb hefted it when it was ready and made sure it was not a heavy load for the little girl. Though she had been hauling wood for Hestor and had gotten much stronger while she was gone, he did not want her to carry heavy burdens.

He was almost done packing the furs when he picked up a bearskin he had tanned some time ago. He had shot the black bear hanging around the cabin one night. He threw the black fur over his shoulders, raised his arms and pretended to growl and chase Kuskusky playfully.

She laughed and growled right back at him, demanding, "Go away, Brother Bear!" Amelia stopped what she was doing when she saw Zeb looking like a half-man, half bear, and suddenly remembered the words she had heard Tamataunee's apparition say to her so long ago. That was the night she had a frightening vision about a bear trying to get into their shelter in the hollow tree stump. Tamataunee had appeared in her dream and told her, *'It is okay, let him have you. He just wants to wrap his arms around you.'* Now she understood.

Zeb had been trapping well over a year without making a trip to the buyer. He had several bundles of pelts. Regretfully, he had to leave some furs behind and just take the most valuable ones. The raccoon and woodchuck were common and would not bring much money, so they were set aside. Someone will move into the cabin when they see it is abandoned, and they can have them. It made him sad to leave the home he had built with his first wife, Bridgette, but he believed a settler who needed it would take it over. Knowing that he was probably passing it on to someone in need, most likely a young soldier, eased his unhappiness at losing it. He had gained so much these last few years. He had learned how to live again after Bridgette had died. With Amelia and Kuskusky, he had found a more profound love and purpose in his life. She had given him a reason to live and had literally saved his life when he would have died pinned beneath that tree.

He owed her much and would do anything for her, including abandoning the homestead he had built. He looked around wistfully at the fireplace he had built from stones he had hauled from the fields and creek and the hand-hewn mantle carved from pine. He remembered the day Bridgette placed the blue bottle on the windowsill and all the good and bad memories he had of his place, and then he pulled the door closed behind him.

CHAPTER 8

ZEB SET OFF IN A SOUTHWESTERLY direction with Kuskusky walking behind him and Amelia a few steps behind her. "We will be reaching the shore far below Reverend Vickery's settlement, so we should be safe from them finding us," he told Amelia. "Keep looking around and be alert though. So much has changed with new people moving here and claiming land. I hope we do not have any surprises coming across strangers and that my buyer is still at Newtown."

He had formulated a plan. He was not sure Amelia would go along with it and had not told her yet. He thought he might build a new homestead. They were both still young, and he had done it before. It had been grueling labor to cut down the trees and build the cabin they were leaving, but Amelia had shown Zeb she could handle hard work like that. But would she want too? She had talked so often about going on to the land of the Cayuga.

Walking was difficult for the three with all that they were carrying. Zeb's load of furs and traps was piled high above his pack basket, plus he carried his ax, and his rifle was slung over his shoulder. He checked Amelia's load to be sure she was not carrying too much weight. He remained concerned about her health; it had taken her so long to be well enough to travel. She had relapsed so often from that Swamp Fever that almost took her life. He did not want to jeopardize her health in any way and bring on another setback.

They kept up a steady pace, only stopping a few times to get a drink and catch their breath. They saw rabbit, turkey, elk, and deer. Another time, he would have stopped and shot one for meat, but not now. The three had covered quite a distance by evening, even walking at the pace they must for Kuskusky to keep up with them. Amelia was so glad her daughter was a strong, resilient girl and loved the outdoors. Zeb was going to make them a lean-to shelter that night amongst thick white pines, but the wind was picking up, and they heard thunder rumbling not far away. A strong storm was quickly bearing down on them, and it would be there soon. Looking around, he could not see a place to shelter near them. "We need to get under a big pine tree right away and sit with our backs to the trunk or we are going to get wet," he told them.

He picked out a massive pine that would offer some shelter for them with its limbs laden with thick clusters of green needles and lots of small brushy pines around its base. Unlike the roots of an oak tree that go straight down to the water and become a rod to attract lightning, the roots of a pine tree fan out and are less likely to draw a strike. At least that is what Zeb hoped as the violent storm came closer and closer with brilliant flashes of light and loud rolling thunder. A couple of years before, he had seen lightning strike a tree and split it completely in two from top to bottom. Then it exploded instantly into a fiery torch. Even though he was a grown man, it had been frightening to see such power. The temperature dropped several degrees and they huddled close together, facing outwards around the trunk. Vesper birds, which usually sang in the evening along with the other sounds of crickets and tree frogs, were silent as the storm approached. Only the sound of howling wind, creaking trees, and booming thunder could be heard now. Kuskusky sat tight next to Amelia. Before the sky opened with torrential rain, Zeb had given them some beaver pelts for cover.

"These will help keep the rain off you," he had told them. The storm arrived as a loud, unwelcome visitor barging into their space. It raged around them, moving and blowing the pine boughs of their sheltering tree and let the rain come in on them at times.

It was a violent storm, and at one point, the thunder was so deafening they could not hear each other's voices and bright lightning flashed at the same time, so they knew the beast was right over them. Then the large hail started falling. Hail so big it bounced on the ground, and when the lightning flashed again and lit up the darkness, the ground was white where it was piling up. They huddled together on a slight rise at the base of the pine, and water on the ground started backing up, threatening to get them wet. Amelia tucked her feet under her and hugged Kuskusky even closer. She wondered why the ancestors were so angry. The wind was still very powerful, and they heard trees nearby snapping off, falling, and crashing. Zeb thought about the tree that had fallen on him and hoped he had picked a place safe for them all. He wished he had found a cave or shelter under a big rock ledge, but all they had around them at the time the storm hit was trees. The hail finally stopped, switching to driving rain and then finally subsided along with the wind. The limbs of the tree they were under stopped swaying and making noises and became quiet. Amelia checked on Kuskusky, who was sound asleep in her arms. It felt so good to be holding her daughter again. She was right where she was supposed to be with her mother.

"Are you still dry?" Zeb asked quietly, not wanting to wake Kuskusky.

"Yes, Zeb, the pelts shed the rain and kept us warm like you said," she answered and yawned. It had been a hard day, and now she was extremely tired like Kuskusky.

"The rain has washed away any trail we may have left," he told her. "That is a blessing."

They had done so much walking to rescue Kuskusky and now striking out on this journey to the lake. Soon all three were sound asleep beneath the sheltering arms of Brother Pine.

They awoke early and stepped out from under the limbs of the pine to see several trees near them had been blown down or broken off during the violent storm. Leaves had been ripped from limbs by the powerful winds and hail and lay torn and scattered on the ground.

The sun, however, was shining bright, and the air smelled fresh as if the earth had just scrubbed itself clean.

Zeb led them on their way again. He had taken his furs to Newtown more than once, so he knew the woods well where he was traveling, although Amelia did not see any marked trail before them. He had used his experience to go off in a diagonal direction from his cabin towards Seneca Lake, where he had hidden his canoe. He planned to take Amelia and Kuskusky by water down the lake and then walk on to Newtown when they could not travel by boat anymore. The terrain was steeply graded downward now as it pitched toward the lake from the mountaintop, and Zeb was following a deer trail to the water. He had kept a sharp eye out for any natives or settlers and avoided any place he thought they might encounter them. A couple of times, they had heard shots far away, and Zeb thought they were probably from settlers shooting game. He avoided going anywhere near them. He did not want any trouble and trusted no one now after his experience with the Reverend Vickery and his wife, Hestor. He had misjudged them so much.

They pushed on down the mountainside and descended further until they finally came across a stream that flowed to the lake. They rested a short while at the top of it and had some dried, smoked meat to eat and drank the cold water from the stream flowing over the grey slate rocks. Kuskusky was doing remarkably well for a young child and was keeping up with Zeb and Amelia while walking and carrying her burden. Zeb and Amelia watched as Kuskusky took her moccasins off and waded into a shallow pool. She laughed when small minnows swam around her toes and tickled them. Zeb and Amelia were both mentally wondering, *how can I keep this child safe from harm by others?* It saddened them to know that Kuskusky had been born into a world where one race treated another so cruelly without even knowing them.

Just then, Kuskusky stepped on some slippery green moss, lost her footing, and with a big splash, sat down abruptly in the cold pool. They laughed at the surprised look on Kuskusky's face, and she laughed too and started splashing water at both. Zeb became concerned at the noise they were making and told her it was time to get back on the trail. Amelia helped Kuskusky stand up and put on her moccasins. They carefully descended beside the stream while being alert and listening intently. They had no idea what they might find on the shore.

Zeb could easily be mistaken for a hostile with his animal skin clothing, and he was carrying a gun. Amelia and Kuskusky both looked like natives with their dark braided hair, Indian clothing, and moccasins. After all the conflicts in the area, they could be considered hostiles by any settlers seeing them. Zeb kept thinking about where they were going and feared what reaction they might get when they met others. Would they get fired upon? Just as he was thinking about that danger, without any warning, a bullet whistled just past Zeb's head. They all reacted by hitting the ground and laying as flat as they could.

"Do not come any closer!" a voice shouted at them, "or I will shoot every damn one of you!"

Zeb raised his head slightly, trying to see who the voice belonged to. Another shot whizzed past his head. That was two misses. This person is either just trying to scare them or is a lousy shot. Zeb figured out the direction the shot came from and motioned Amelia and Kuskusky to stay low and hidden where they were. He would sneak around and get behind the shooter.

All was quiet for some tense moments, then the voice shouted. "Did you hear me? Or don't you speak English? I will shoot you and leave your bodies for the animals to tear apart, I mean it! Do not come any closer!" Just as he finished that last warning, Zeb was behind him and pushed the barrel of his rifle against the shooter's back. He was just a young boy, not more than fourteen years old. He stood up and dropped his gun at once. Zeb could tell he was terribly frightened of him.

"Turn around," he ordered and then, "why are you shooting at us, boy? We have not done anything to you!"

"You speak English," the boy uttered, confused. "I thought you were savages sneaking up on me wanting to take my scalp."

Disgusted, Zeb told him, "You could have killed any one of us, you damn fool, and we have a child with us. Don't ever fire on anyone until you know their intentions. Do you hear me, boy? It is a damn good thing you are a terrible shot!"

Embarrassed and afraid, he answered, "Yes, sir, I am sorry."

Zeb checked around and did not see anyone else with the boy. "Are you alone?" he asked. The youth did not answer right away, and Zeb asked again louder, "Are you alone, boy!"

"Yes, I was going to shoot some squirrels for supper," he told Zeb.

"Well, I don't think any squirrel was in any danger of losing its life the way you aim. Just where is your cabin?" Zeb asked, and the youth pointed northward, off into the woods. "Now, this is what is going to happen," he told the boy. "We are going down to the lake and get in our canoe and leave. I am taking your rifle so you cannot shoot us if you still feel like doing something stupid. I will leave it down by the shore. If you try to get it before we are out of sight in our canoe, I will shoot you. I don't want to, but if you try to hurt us again, I will shoot, and I am a good marksman and do not miss like you. You stay right here until we are gone, and you will be safe. Think about that and be smart about it! We just want to pass through here with no more trouble. You got that?"

Shaken, the boy nodded his head 'yes.'

Zeb motioned Amelia and Kuskusky to get up from hiding and move on down towards the lake. He followed behind them, carrying his rifle as well as the boy's and scanning the woods around them. When they reached the shoreline, Amelia stayed back with Kuskusky hidden among brush and trees. Zeb recognized where they were and went right over to an area thick with willow brush. Hidden snug against a large old log was his overturned canoe and paddle. He dragged it out and carried it to the shore after checking first to see if there was any activity nearby. He told Amelia to load the canoe with the pelts and other burdens they were carrying while he kept watching. Then they stepped into the boat and sat down. Zeb put the boy's rifle in plain sight on the shore and then pushed the canoe out further before jumping into it himself. He used his paddle to push the boat into even deeper water, so they were floating freely and then pointed the bow southward down the lake. He paddled far out from the shore. He did not want any prying eyes seeing them clearly in the canoe. They were all silent as the canoe moved along. Zeb looked back at where they had launched the canoe. The young boy was on the shore, picking up his rifle and staring at them. Zeb hoped that was the last trouble he had from the settlers. He did not want anyone shooting near his precious cargo.

The only sound they heard now was the liquid swish of water being pushed by the paddle as Zeb stroked the surface with a regular rhythm. The wind was at their backs and they were moving southward at a good pace. Zeb kept the boat well out from the lakeshore. Amelia scanned the distance shoreline looking for something familiar from the time she had lived along it with Tamataunee and Mahonoy. All she saw was new settler's cabins with smoke coming from chimneys. It had not taken settlers long to move onto the lands of the Seneca and claim them as their own. *How many more strangers would come?* She wondered. She was shocked to see crops growing among the stumps of the ruined Seneca orchards and whole areas cleared of the apple, pear, and cherry trees that she and others had picked fruit from just a few years earlier.

Where had all the Seneca gone? Had the soldiers killed them all? Surely some others like herself must have survived. She felt a terrible catch in her heart and sadness when she recognized the spot by the stream where Tamataunee and Mahonoy had been killed the day the soldiers charged into their village. It is all gone. The longhouses, the Seneca cabins, their orchards, gardens, and any signs of them ever living there are gone. Did the whites make any Seneca and Lenape who escaped the carnage their slaves, and do they have to work for them to survive like Hestor told us? She thought of Kuskusky's future and wondered what her fate in life would be. *Where do Kuskusky and I belong now?*

Kuskusky was enjoying being out on the water. She was happily looking over the side of the canoe to see fish beneath or watched ducks bobbing on the waves. Amelia had to scold her to sit still. Kuskusky did not know how to swim, and Amelia was afraid she was going to fall overboard with all her moving around. Zeb told Amelia that after they reached the end of the lake, they would follow the stream as far as they could navigate it and then continue on foot to Matthias Hollenbeck's Trading Post.

The wind sped them along, and soon, they were at the inlet of Seneca Lake, where a large stream continued into a narrow valley of marshes spreading out on all sides. Canada geese, mallards, and beautiful wood ducks swam curiously near them, then turned away and returned to the tall bulrushes growing at the edge. This was a flood plain area, and there were no settler's cabins in sight. Muskrats sat atop their grassy brown mounds in green cattails and stared warily at them before diving into the safety of the water. An osprey spread its wings wide and soared over the stream, looking for fish to capture. Deer that had been eating lush grass growing in the marshy area bounded away, back into the depths of the woods as Zeb's canoe approached where they were browsing. These waters flowed northward back to the lake. It was the inlet to Seneca Lake, not the outlet, so the further south they traveled, the shallower it became until they were forced to leave the canoe. Zeb pulled their vessel up onto firm ground. Amelia helped him drag it out of sight, and he marked a tree so he could find it again when needed. Once again, they strapped their burdens of furs and necessities onto their backs and started walking south.

The canoe travel had been restful on the lake and through the marshy area. Now, they were walking on firmer land, and Zeb was choosing his path carefully. He still wanted to avoid contact with anyone until he had to do his trading, but the closer they got to Hollenbeck's Trading Post, the more homesteads they saw. The soldiers in General Sullivan's army had been so impressed by the beauty around Seneca Lake that they had chosen to come back and settle there. Many had been granted land for their service in routing the natives from the land belonging to the Seneca. The whole area consisted of thousands of acres and was now called the Military Tract. It was being converted to farmland and lumbering. Most of the beaver and other desirable fur-bearing animals had already been depleted so much that trapping was no longer a dependable income. Deer and fish were heavily harvested also. The meat was salted, packed into barrels and sent to the nearest town for sale or to the lodging places for meals.

Zeb had been fortunate to get so many good pelts. But his way of life was disappearing. What he saw of the landscape and homesteads he traveled through made him sure of that. Before long, they saw Hollenbeck's place off in the distance. They walked on, and Amelia could see the trading post was a two-story clapboard sided building. She studied the structure as they neared it. She had never seen a two-story building with a second level of rooms. The white store had a porch with square pillars that ran across the front. It was littered with barrels and boxes. Farm tools leaned against its front wall. A large sign over the porch stated, "Hollenbeck's Mercantile," and beneath that were the words "Dry Goods & Trading Post." The store sold whatever a homesteader might need.

A couple of men looking like farmers sat on wooden crates and turned their heads and stared when Zeb, Amelia, and Kuskusky stepped onto the porch. They never offered a greeting, but Zeb said, "Hello," and they slowly nodded their heads at him while continuing to stare. Amelia was so unsure of these white men and the strange environment that she held on tight to Kuskusky's hand and stayed half-hidden behind Zeb's back. A bell jingled over the door as Zeb opened it and stepped into the dimly lit room. Amelia and Kuskusky were tight behind him and stepped inside as well. They all stood together for a moment to let their eyes to get used to the filtered light coming through the wavy windowpanes. No other lights lit the room. Lanterns were saved for the evening in homes and shops. The whale oil used in them was too valuable to burn during the day.

The owners and proprietors were Mathias Hollenbeck and his wife, who lived upstairs over the mercantile. Mrs. Hollenbeck was busy helping some ladies shopping for yard goods to sew for clothing. She was showing them the latest gingham that had just arrived from the mills in England. The women turned and stared at Zeb and Amelia just as the men outside had done. Zeb stood out with his trapper's clothing, and so did Amelia and Kuskusky the way they were dressed. One of the ladies looked at them and uttered something to the others. They all shook their heads in agreement. Neither Zeb nor Amelia could make out what her comment was but knew it was not friendly. The women turned their backs on them and continued stroking and admiring the fabric Mrs. Hollenbeck was holding out to them.

Zeb went over to the counter where Mr. Hollenbeck was standing and told him he had furs he wanted to sell. Mr. Hollenbeck recognized him right away and was pleased to see him. He stuck out his hand and greeted Zeb warmly. He had done business with Zeb before and knew what a good trapper he was. Zeb's pelts were always cleaned of every bit of fat and flesh and stretched and preserved exactly the way they should be, not done sloppily like most of the new settlers. Zeb knew what he was doing and was incredibly skilled at it. His pelts would bring Hollenbeck good money when he resold them to the Hudson Bay Fur Company. The price of fur had gone up due to the game getting scarcer and the demand. Hollenbeck was happy at the prospect of getting some from Zeb. Beaver hats were still wanted by many, and women desired more mink, ermine, and fine furs than ever before. Hollenbeck was happy to have Zeb in his store. The squaw and her child were not entirely so welcome.

When Kuskusky started looking around and touching all the marvelous and strange items she had never seen before, Hollenbeck stopped examining the furs Zeb had and scolded her for touching things. "Do not let that child touch anything," he told Amelia. "I don't want any of my merchandise to come up missing." Amelia drew Kuskusky close and held onto her hand as they continued to look at the merchandise in the glass cabinets and shelves. Amelia was just as amazed as Kuskusky by what she saw there.

Zeb and Matthias Hollenbeck were counting pelts and haggling over their value, and then they agreed on a price and shook hands. Hollenbeck went to his safe and handed Zeb some money. Zeb tucked it away inside his jacket and then went to Amelia, gave her some coins, and told her to buy something for herself and Kuskusky, he had some more talking to do with Mr. Hollenbeck in the back room.

Looking down at the strange coins in her hand, Amelia told him, "Zeb, I do not know what these coins are worth, or know how to count money."

He realized that she had never had to use money for anything while living with the Indians and spoke to Mrs. Hollenbeck, "My woman is going to buy something. You will take good care of her, won't you, Mrs. Hollenbeck? We also need flour, sugar, lard, and eggs. I have a real hunger for some eggs. I will settle up with you when they are done shopping." Mrs. Hollenbeck agreed to help her, and Zeb gave Amelia orders to buy something, he did not care what. It was the first time Zeb had called Amelia "my woman," and Amelia liked the sound of it. As she gazed around the mercantile, she and Kuskusky felt as if they had discovered a cave of treasures.

There were so many wonderful things to choose from. There were cards of beautiful shiny buttons made from disks of cut seashells. A rack with rolls of patterned ribbons in several colors caught their attention, and they felt the smooth silkiness of the materials they were made from. There were gleaming tin and copper utensils, interesting books with pictures and big lidded jars of colorfully wrapped candies, and envelopes that held seeds had drawings of flowers and vegetables on them. One shelf along the back wall displayed white porcelain dishes painted with intricate dark blue patterns. There were leather shoes, combs, brushes and jars, and bottles of medicines with names like 'Swamp-Root Elixir' and 'Strength and Liver Tonic.' Pots and pans hung from hooks, and they saw razors with leather strops for sharpening them and shaving brushes for men in cups filled with soap. Right next to them was mustache wax and hair tonic guaranteed to grow thicker hair. So many strange and unusual things.

Amelia chose some ribbons and a couple of bars of sweet-smelling soap. Kuskusky was fascinated by the glass jars of assorted candies and wanted to buy a few. It was hard to get Mrs. Hollenbeck's attention to make their purchases, though. Amelia stood at the counter for a long time before Mrs. Hollenbeck finally left the ladies to wait on her. She seemed bothered and annoyed, and she was not friendly. Amelia wished

Zeb would hurry and come back into the room. Mrs. Hollenbeck was making her feel uncomfortable and unwelcome by her attitude, and she wanted to get Kuskusky out of that place.

The bell over the door jingled again, and they turned to see who was entering the store. A woman was supporting an elderly lady by the elbow who walked next to her. The old woman was bent with age and used a cane. Soon it was apparent to those watching that she was also blind.

"Why hello ladies, you have not visited us in some time," Mrs. Hollenbeck greeted them warmly. It was not the same reception Amelia had gotten. "What brings you here today, Mrs. Chandler?"

The taller woman answered as she continued to lead the elder into the store. "Well, you know I like to take her out every so often. Take her someplace besides the house so she can feel some fresh air and talk to people. Besides, she loves that rose-scented soap you have, and she is out of it. That makes her really pouty." Amelia looked down at the soap she had bought. It had a drawing of a rose on its wrapper.

"Stop talking about me like I am a child. I can take care of myself," the older woman said. "Just point me to where the soap is in this place. I used to make the best soap for Cornelius when I was younger. Better than the rose soap they sell here." She continued talking, "Now I cannot do anything like making soap. I hate being so old. I do not know why the Lord did not take me away a long time ago. I should be dead right now, not a bother to anyone to escort me around places. It almost killed me when those Indians took me, but I survived." She shook her finger in the air.

In all the years since she had escaped from the Lenape, Ina had hardened her heart against all Indians. They were responsible for her son Rubin's death and for taking her daughter from her. She hated and despised every one of them and wished all Indians were not just gone from where she lived, but dead.

Mrs. Hollenbeck spoke up, "Now, Ina, do not talk about being gone. You know we like to see you here in our store."

Ahmeya, hearing the names Ina and Cornelius, looked closely at the old woman. Could it possibly be who she hoped it was? She had not seen her since she was nine years old. That was so many years ago. Then she stepped closer and asked her, "Is your name truly Ina, Ina Benjamin, perhaps?"

Trying to see the person who was speaking through the clouded lenses of her eyes, the older woman turned her face towards Amelia and spoke, "Why yes, young lady."

Amelia continued, "Cornelius is your husband, is he not?" Amelia asked, full of emotion.

"Yes, but how did you know that?" The old woman was confused.

"Mother . . . ," Amelia choked on her words, "Mother, I am Amelia, your daughter." She hurried to her side with Kuskusky. Everyone stopped what they were doing to witness the unusual reunion. Hearing what Amelia said, Ina's knees buckled beneath her, and Mrs. Chandler and Amelia helped her sit on a wooden chair nearby.

"Amelia . . . Amelia, my sweet daughter, I knew you were still alive, and I would see you again someday. Come close my daughter and let me touch you, for I cannot see any longer. Cataracts have clouded my eyes. Amelia went close, and they hugged and kissed each other.

"Did those savages hurt you?" Ina asked, holding on to Amelia's hands. "Are you okay, do you live nearby? How did you escape?" She asked several questions one after another without even waiting for an answer, and then she talked on. "I hate and despise those heathen barbarians and would kill every one of them, I do not care who they are if I could put my hands on them for tearing our family apart, I would kill them. Oh, I wish Cornelius and Christopher were here to see you."

"Where are they, Mother?" Amelia asked.

A sad look came over Ina's face and visibly shaken; she fell silent.

Mrs. Chandler, the tall woman with her, spoke. "Oh dear, I am so sorry to tell you they were both killed in an accident at the mill. Cornelius put in a new steam-powered saw and something went wrong. Steam kept building up, and they could not get it under control. It blew up along with the fire in the burner and set the whole mill ablaze. They were trapped and did not get away in time. The doctor believed they were probably knocked out by the explosion and did not know what was happening to them. It was dreadfully sad. After that, I offered to take care of her, and Ina moved in with my husband and I. Her eyesight was already fading and months later, she lost it completely. We do not mind taking care of her though, we enjoy having her in our house, she is good company for me. And my husband was able to build a new mill right on that same property."

Amelia was saddened to know her father and brother were dead. She had wanted to see them even though years earlier they had taken part in the massacre of her village. She still loved them, and some of her bitter feelings had softened with time. She was older and understood now that war forced men to set aside their humanity and do horrible things that they would never do in another situation. They became animals trained to attack by leaders driven to win for what they believe is a good cause.

Kuskusky tugged at Amelia's hand and asked if she could have a piece of her candy now. Curious, Mrs. Chandler spoke up and asked Amelia, "Who is this child you have with you?"

"A child?" Ina asked, eager to hear the answer.

"Yes, Mother, this is my daughter Kuskusky," and she pushed a reluctant Kuskusky towards her.

"Come close child, so I can touch you, I cannot see anymore." Ina reached out, and Mrs. Chandler guided her hand so she could touch Kuskusky standing in front of her. Ina gently stroked her hair and felt her braids. "Why, you braid her hair up just like I did yours, Amelia." Tears started running down Ina's face as she continued to touch the young girl's cheeks. "She is a beautiful child I can tell." Ina reached out and drew Kuskusky closer to her and kissed her forehead. "Oh, you beautiful little girl." Ina was kissing and hugging her more. Kuskusky squirmed at the unusual affection from a stranger. "What did you say you named her?" she asked Amelia.

"Her name is Kuskusky, Mother. I call her Kuskusky."

"That is such an unusual name, it sounds foreign," Ina answered, not realizing that it was an Indian name and Kuskusky was dark-skinned. Then she went on, "Thank the Lord you escaped from those savages and married a settler," Ina said, "I never stopped praying for you. What is your husband's name?" she asked.

Amelia hesitated. She wanted to tell her Mother her first love and father of the child she was now kissing was a Seneca brave named Tamataunee. Kuskusky had his blood, and she was proud of that, but she did not tell her. What good would it do?

Instead, she answered, "Zebulon," his name is Zebulon Warfle. He is here right now selling furs to Mr. Hollenbeck. Just as she said that Zeb came over to her side. She introduced Ina to him, "Mother, this is my husband, Zeb." Zeb was surprised at what she just declared. It was the first time she had referred to him that way.

Ina spoke up, "I am so glad you married my sweet Amelia and had a child with her." It was dead silent in the room. Anyone with good eyes could plainly tell Kuskusky was not his child, but no one contradicted the elderly woman. Mrs. Chandler stiffened her back and regarded them both with a stern face and no glimpse of compassion. The silence was painfully awkward.

"I have got my business done here," Zeb told her, "it is time to leave Amelia."

Ina pleaded, "Must you go now, we just found each other after all those years. Please come visit me where I live with Mrs. Chandler." Then turning towards her caretaker, she asked: "Would you tell them the way to your house so they may visit?"

Mrs. Chandler gave directions, but they were vague. She insisted she would like a message sent ahead of time to be aware of their visit, and she was terribly sorry, but there would be no room for them to stay with her overnight. It was apparent they were not welcome. Ina gave Kuskusky a warm goodbye hug, kissed her cheeks again, and told her to grow up strong like her mother and mind her Papa. Amelia hugged her mother lovingly and said goodbye. It was a long affectionate hug, for she felt she might never see her again.

Then Zeb put his arm around her waist and held Kuskusky's hand as they slowly left the store to the sound of Ina saying, "Goodbye, my sweet Amelia, goodbye, my sweet little Kuskusky. Grandma loves you."

The small family walked further down the street to a barn with the sign Blacksmith and Livery over the big open doors. Smells of a smoldering coal fire and sweaty horses were coming from the interior. Zeb told Amelia and Kuskusky to wait for him and went in to talk to the owner.

"Stay close," he warned. "and come and get me if anyone troubles you." Amelia and Kuskusky sat down on a bench against the wall. Kuskusky was having a great time sitting there in the sunshine, swinging her feet back and forth. She looked around at the cluster of strange buildings and people going about their daily routines, and it was all so exciting for her. She was totally unaware of how different she looked from the other inhabitants and the unfair judgments of so many living there. A stray dog came up to them, and she jumped off the bench to kneel and pet it. The dog licked her face eagerly as if she were a sweet treat, and Kuskusky laughed at its wet kisses. Then it knocked her over with its friendly greeting. When Kuskusky sat back up giggling, the dog sat down beside her.

Kuskusky put her arm around the shaggy yellow-colored dog and asked Amelia, "Mother, can we keep him?"

"He probably belongs to someone else, Kuskusky," she told her disappointed daughter. They heard horses whinny followed by the sound of their footsteps and Zeb came out of the barn riding a horse and leading two others. Amelia and Kuskusky both jumped up in surprise.

"We are not walking all over the woods and countryside anymore," he told them, "climb up there, woman." He smiled and pointed at the other saddled horse. Amelia smiled back at him, lifted Kuskusky up onto the horse, and climbed up after her. The remaining horse had provisions and staples they had bought at the mercantile.

"You can afford these horses, Zeb?" she asked.

"Yes, I can, and that is not all Amelia. I sold my cabin and the land that goes with it to Mr. Hollenbeck. He deals in land grants too. Gave me good money for it. I do not want to live there anymore with people like Reverend Vickery and his wife Hestor, who want to take our little girl from us. Besides, game is getting so scarce with the new people movin' in and takin' it all. You, me, and Kuskusky are going further west over the mountains and are buildin' a new cabin for us. We may even go as far as the Ohio country. What do you think of that, Kuskusky? Do you want to ride a horse and see new things?"

Kuskusky smiled at Zeb and shook her head eagerly. Then she looked down at the friendly dog who was sitting close by whining at them and wagging its tail. "Momma, can we take him?" The owner of the Livery was standing in the doorway and heard her pleading.

"You are welcome to that mutt if you want him. He hangs around here gettin' in the way all the time," he told Kuskusky, who smiled wide.

Zeb called the dog closer, and he came right to him, wagging his tail. "He is a friendly one. Thanks, we will add a dog to our family." Zeb tipped his hat goodbye to the Livery owner and thanked him.

Amelia looked at Zeb's face as he sat there, holding the reins ready to guide them all onward. He twisted in his saddle and asked her. "Are you ready to go, Amelia? I know you wanted to be with the Cayuga." Zeb studied her eyes for a sign of what she wanted to do. She would have a more comfortable life in the north with the Cayuga and Kuskusky would be raised by people like her own heritage. He hoped he would not lose them, he wanted to have both Amelia and Kuskusky in his life. They had given him a reason to live and be happy again. He asked, "What do you think, Amelia? You can take that horse and the one with the provisions and head north to the Cayuga right now if you want to. I owe you that much and more. Do you still want to be with people like you and Kuskusky?"

Amelia thought hard about what Zeb was offering her. Now she could leave with Kuskusky and have a real chance of reaching the Great Council Meeting Place. She had no idea what lay ahead of her if she stayed with this trapper. He had been a difficult person at times, and they would have to do a lot of work to build a place to live again. Zeb had sheltered and protected them when she was all alone and needed help. He had stayed by her side and nursed her back to health when she was deadly ill and rescued her daughter from Hestor and the Reverend.

To keep them safe, he left all he had accomplished. Now, looking at his rugged face, she saw the love in his eyes and knew he truly cared for them both.

Amelia looked back at him and said, "I found someone like me, Zeb. Let's leave this place."

Zeb smiled warmly and silently nodded his head at her. Then he tapped the ribs of his horse with his heels. Amelia and Kuskusky followed as they headed west towards the distant mountains. Amelia was thinking, *Someday, I will tell Kuskusky more about her brave Seneca father, Tamataunee, her Lenape grandmother, Mahonoy, and about this kind and loving man, Zeb, and what he has done for us. Someday, after we build our homestead in those far mountains. Sometime soon, when we are living with the spirits of the woods again where we all belong.*

THE END

ABOUT THE AUTHOR

DORIS WILBUR is the author of three novels, *A Lenape Legacy, Riding the Float*, and *A Lenape Captive: Ahmeya*. She lives at a small lake in rural New York State and writes about historical events and issues of our contemporary times. Her stories are infused with nature and give you a real sense of place while taking you on an adventure filled with challenges, humor, romance, and life altering choices.

Doris spent much of her career as a commercial artist and award watercolor artist. She was a public-school teacher also, but behind the scenes she always wrote. She believes her artistic abilities help her visualize the scenes in her novels and give detailed descriptions that bring them to life for the reader. She has worked for newspapers, advertising agencies, school systems and has a fine art business.

She and her husband Jerry raised five children and have lived in rural New York State, the mountains of Pennsylvania, near Washington DC and in a small town in central Florida. She has worked in busy and congested large cities as well as living a peaceful country life in a small town.

Doris graduated summa cum laude from Mansfield University of Pennsylvania where she studied Creative Writing, Botany and Art Education. Now, she and her husband enjoy life at a private lake surrounded by woods and nature where she continues to write and paint.